LAURA & Mr SOLIS,

Rent–free

Virginie PAQUIER

Translated from the French novel

"Offre Logement Contre Menus Services"

by Emilie Grenon

L'ENVERS DES CORPS

Novel, 2013

Mes Vérités à dire, et à contredire

Collection of columns, 2014

OFFRE LOGEMENT CONTRE MENUS SERVICES

Novel, 2015

LA JOLIE VIE DE MELANIE

Novel, 2016

DEUXIEME ETAGE, RAYON HOMMES

Novel, 2016

ELLE M'AVAIT DIT...

Novel, 2016

NOEUD DE VIPERES DANS L'HERBE VERTE

Novel, 2016

At 34 years old, I am a fulfilled woman. I am rich. I travel around the whole world. I frequent the best restaurants and the most beautiful places in Paris. I meet talented, creative, fascinating people. My private life is extraordinary, exciting - beyond my expectations.

Yet, I come from a modest, rural family – an insular environment, without ambition, hemmed in its petty mind. My story is not typical. It is a story of encounters, coincidences, opportunities taken against all reason and contrary to my upbringing. In my childhood and then in my teenage dreams, I could never have had imagined becoming the person I am today. I am neither proud nor ashamed. I am myself, and without any remorse.

CHAPTER I

We were almost twenty years old, Greg and I, and we were in love. From the beginning, growing up in our family homes, we lived just a couple of streets apart, close to the city of Biarritz in France's south west.

The sea, the blue sky. It was August and, like every year, we were sunbathing and talking about the future, on the beach of Port-Vieux, happy to at last be able to take advantage of the holiday, well deserved after a month of hard work. Lying there on our bellies, we had to muster an effort to just free our mouths from our towels, with laziness making small-talk hard.

- So, Laura, how do you reckon we should organise ourselves for September? Are you going to look for a room during the week and then come back every weekend? Or every second weekend?
- I think we don't have much choice. I start my first courses on the third and I know nobody in Paris, so tonight I'll go online to find a room.
- We're not going to see each other a lot.
- No, especially because I will have lots to study during the weekend, so…
- Well, it's only for two years – it'll be fine.
- Yeah, it will be fine.

I had to fight to be admitted at this business school! Without much in the way of finances, I had to jostle and be pushy to obtain enough instalments for my university fees. Without this, it would have been impossible to make a budget, including a room there in Paris or in the near suburbs, as well as the daily expenses for the next two years. But this was the only school which offered classes in 'art and culture of the world'. And that was my dream, for me, even coming from a working-class family. To travel, to meet intellectuals and artists, to become an international art dealer - that was how I imagined my professional future. Greg, who also came from the same social background, encouraged me with his usual enthusiasm. He had chosen to become a sports trainer and got accepted at a local university for a minimum three years degree.

We had been together for four years, happy and enthusiastic about several common passions like surfing, cinema, cooking and reading…

- We will have a beautiful house next…
- …with dogs and a garden full of flowers.
- It will have to be huge, so that we can invite everybody!

Back home at my parents, I went on the internet searching rent websites for private individuals. It would be a good thing for my wallet if I could avoid paying fees to a rental agency. From the start, my search ran into difficulties, as there were so many different kinds of offers, and the prices looked completely excessive to me. I knew well enough that renting in Paris would be expensive, but at that point it was looking almost impossible. Four hundred euros for a simple room with toilets on the landing… Yet my budget was just two hundred fifty euros, and even then, only after getting rid of any unnecessary expenses. When I entered this amount as my first research criterion, the only results to come up were some really doubtful offers, in some questionable quarters that were too far away from my school. After many hours of meticulous research, my back aching and tight with frustration, I thought I better postpone it until the day after.

In the morning, Greg gave me a call.

- So? Did you find anything?
- No, not yet. Everything is stupidly expensive. I don't even know where I should look to find places that actually fit my budget. Perhaps at a dormitory or a youth hostel? Something like that.
- Are you kidding? You will need a quiet and comfortable place to focus on all the work you'll have to do! You'll need a proper room if you want to do well.
- But I really can't borrow money for the rent! How am I going to do this?
- Alright, how about I come over this afternoon and we'll do it together? How are the others doing?

Greg was right. I couldn't be the only working-class student coming from a country town to study in Paris. Although…

He arrived around three o'clock and at eight o'clock we were still browsing and looking for every opportunity. Flat, sub-lease, room sharing, we must have called around fifty times, but no luck. The rent was either too high, or it was too far away, or else the room had just been rented. Everything seemed to be taken very quickly or at least those which fit the smallest budgets, like my own. It was driving us nuts! I really only had one solution left: to travel up to Paris myself, to have a look at the adverts and be able to hurry and see the landlords directly…. It was the only way to make the most of my slim chances. Without knowing the city, it would be a kind of a sport, but the landlords obviously didn't have to move a finger to find candidates, even in quarters they might have considered as remote and out of the way.

My mother, who felt powerless not knowing what to do to help me, suggested that Greg have dinner with us. And so we spent some more time talking about it all, going over our weariness again and again like an old-fashioned song.

-	I really have to find something. I won't give up this school just because of rent. It would be so stupid!

-   You're right. So take a ticket to Paris - it surely will be easier up there. We'll pay for the trip, your dad and I.

So, the next morning, I booked a ticket to leave the following day. I would sleep in a cheap hotel for as long it would take, as little time possible, and meanwhile I could continue my investigations, just in case.

Around eleven o' clock, a new online advert drew my attention.

« Offer exchange: share vast and comfortable apartment, ideally situated in Paris 8th *arrondissement*, for minor daily services. »

Reading this passage, I immediately imagined an old lady or an old, lonely and frail wealthy male landlord of a stately familial apartment, who needed help with his shopping, chores and so on… Why not? Of course, I would have to dedicate a lot of time to my studies, but in my spare time, I could well spend it doing these "minor daily services". It would also be a good deed, and surely an interesting experience -there was no doubt about it. I dialled the number. The person answering the phone sounded like a middle aged man, perhaps thirty or forty years old, seemingly in a hurry and hardly talkative. What to think? Perhaps he was probably handicapped or sick and it might have been rude to ask such a question during this first contact. The man confirmed to me his apartment was very well situated, in a quiet quarter, covering an area close to a hundred and fifty square meters, and he was not looking at sub-leasing it for money but for having company, preferably female, someone who could understand him and help him with "minor services".

- Money isn't a problem. You wouldn't have anything to pay. It's ideal for a student.
- But what kind of services are you asking for? I don't know if I would be able to do it.
- Oh, nothing very difficult. I would only ask you to talk to me according to the way I like.
- … Is that all? But are you sure?
- Yes, absolutely. However, you will have to respect carefully my requests every day.
- Well, listen, I will be in Paris tomorrow. Could we meet there?
- Certainly, it's perfect. I suggest you to come straight to my place. You will see with your own eyes I haven't lied to you about the quality of the apartment.

I was so on my toes that I did not dare to ask for more details or any explanation, because I was afraid he could hang up, but the man had been very evasive. "You would only have to talk to me according to the way I will choose", he had said, or something like that. I didn't quite understand what it was about, but it didn't seem difficult, and I didn't have much choice. I would see when I got there, and anyway, he wouldn't eat me. Maybe he was simply in a hurry, and I was too tense on the phone to understand just what he meant.

After calling Greg to let him inform that I had obtained an appointment, I kept searching nonetheless – in vain – until the evening, and then the next day travelled alone to the capital. This really was an adventure for me. I had only been to Paris two or three times, as a tourist, and to have an entrance interview for my school. I didn't know the city well, but I was doing a good job making my way around on the Paris metro, and it was enough for me to visit apartments.

I arrived at the street that had been indicated to me over the phone and, coming out of the metro, I was completely astounded. The quarter was gorgeous, bordered by a wonderful park, the weather was nice and the Parisians seemed much more relaxed than what people liked to imagine in my town – well, at least for the moment while summer lasts! They were walking in couples, in groups, in joyful pace, satisfaction on their faces. I couldn't resist taking a photo with my cell phone, to send to Greg with a little message « Behold my future quarter! ». He would not believe it.

I came nearer to the address of the building, a beautiful construction, built of dressed stone, with sculpted edges and balconies with wrought iron safety guards. The gate was huge, made of painted wood and equipped with a 'Digi-code' - a real urban princess gate. I rang and a calm, friendly voice answered.

- Is that you, Laura?
- Yes, hello… Sir.
- I will open the gate for you. It is on the third floor, left door.

He definitely was waiting for me, and I was reassured that he hadn't forgotten me. I chose to climb the stairs, rather than take the lift, to better appreciate the broad staircase and the softness of the carpet. The closer I got, the better I could see myself using such a beautiful staircase in such a beautiful place every day. On the second floor, I bumped into a very elegant young woman who greeted me with grace and poise. It took me a moment to respond to her, distracted while admiring her proud bearing. She might well have asked herself what a girl like me, so simply dressed and preferring to take the stairs rather than the lift (which was decorated with sculptures and Art-deco style painted windows), was doing in her building. At last, I reached the third floor, and rang at Mr. Solis' door - the name he gave me on the phone. The heavy door opened, and a man of about thirty held out his hand. He was well dressed, and immediately I noticed his black eyes, above a pure white collar.

- Hello, Laura. Welcome. Come in!
- Hello, Sir. Thanks.
- Have you travelled well? Would you like to drink something?
- With pleasure, thank you very much. Your quarter is more than pleasant.
- See? I haven't lied to you, have I?

We took a seat in the lounge, by my standards an enormous room furnished with great style, on a black leather sofa. I felt a little tense, so small and not fitting in at all with the interior decoration. To help me relax, he offered me a glass of fresh juice, and asked me with interest where I would be studying, and for how long I was thinking of staying in Paris. He presented himself as a charming, refined man, talking calmly and softly, taking time to choose his words. He did not seem sick, and he certainly did not look handicapped nor injured in any way. The school was two metro stations away from the apartment, so no more than a quarter of an hour of travelling, almost from door to door! Unexpectedly lucky. When I finished my glass, my host offered me to show me around the apartment, and it all corresponded exactly with his promises. It was spacious, bright, enriched by attentive decoration. The rooms, three altogether, were furnished in a manner at the same time stylish and sober, with a kitschy touch here and there - a little but not too much. The room which he presented as mine seemed a bit darker, but for the rest, I was already feeling at home. The visit went on with the two bathrooms, both comfortable enough, following by a dressing room adjoining both bedrooms, and a laundry. The floor was parquet, and the ceiling featured subtle mouldings, I had never been inside such a luxurious apartment. It reminded me of the houses featured in those interior decoration magazines that I used to flick through at my aunt's place, Marie, who was thus able to enjoy this luxury that she could not afford in real life. Doubt crept into my mind as we concluded the tour, arriving back at the carpeted marble entry. I needed to have confirmation.

- So, you're offering to share your apartment for free?
- Well… not exactly for free. I'm asking of you something in return, as I told you on the phone.
- Could you explain me again what is it you're precisely expecting me to do? I'm not sure I understood very well.
- Of course. It's very simple: I want you to mistreat me.
- Sorry?
- I want you to insult me, to be sadistic with me.
- I don't understand.
- Every day, when we see each other in this apartment, you will insult me, and you will belittle me. You will behave as a sadist mistress.
- Is that a joke?
- Not at all, it's very serious. I don't ask you to sleep with me, but only to mistreat me through your words.
- This is out of question! You're mad! I'm not interested at all!

Red with embarrassment and anger, I collected my things and left immediately.

In the street, I started walking very fast, hitting the ground with my heel at every step as if it could expel my rage, without knowing where I was going. I felt rigid with disappointment and annoyance, and I needed to stretch my legs, both in order to avoid thinking too much and to get away from this place. After a couple of minutes, I fell onto a bench, breathing out of spite. What the hell just happened? This man was crazy - he did not even seem to be joking, and nor did he try to explain or excuse himself. He just stood there, in front of me, with a completely serious face, as if he were offering me a normal job, as secretary, say. Impossible, insane! Greg would not believe this either. Was that Paris? Weird people who suggest ridiculous things to you with a completely natural look on their face? Why should such a strange story be destined to me? Did it really appear I was suitable to do this kind of thing? Would he have suggested that to any other girl? I was almost ready to feel guilty, to think it was my fault, that somehow because of my behaviour I had encouraged this man to imagine things. Did my clothes let him think I was looking for a dirty sexual adventure? I was wearing a pair of black jeans and a polka dot blouse - nothing seductive according to me. But I had come to this appointment so naively…

How could I imagine someone renting for free in this sort of place? I had certainly been stupid to believe that. Inevitably, it meant I was an easy girl, a bimbo, without principles. What a dummy! Better, actually, that I keep it all to myself, as I was too ashamed and offended. I would tell Greg the person had changed his mind and he had cancelled the appointment. Greg had even replied to my text already, insisting I could not let go of such a great luck!

CHAPTER II

I spent a while calming myself on the bench - a quarter of an hour, maybe longer - before managing to pull myself together. Nothing serious had happened, after all, and no doubt I would see something like that happen again, living in this city for another two years. Anyway, I wasn't a little girl anymore! I slung my bag back over my shoulder and decided to go to my hotel to pick up my keys and grab something to drink. Arriving in the morning I had gone straight to the appointment. Now I had to buy some newspapers and keep searching for a place to rent, as I had planned before. Haunted by this first experience, I was now worried about meeting the other landlords. To encourage myself, I made an effort to focus only on my objective - that was, finding a quiet place located in a convenient part of town and within my budget - that's all. Eating a sandwich, I scanned the offers and found several apartments which might suit me. I took the chance to set three appointments in the late afternoon, places situated in a neighbourhood not far from my school. I was feeling determined as I arrived at the first address – a small independent studio flat of twelve square meters for three hundred and ten euros a month. This price was beyond my budget, but I wanted to know what I could expect at that price. When I arrived, the landlord – looking very normal – explained to me that the studio wasn't in a perfect state, but everything was in line with the safety standards and I shouldn't worry about some aspects of the house and electricity and heating charges, and so on. I might have believed her if I hadn't seen the creeping mould stains which could only be due to a humidity problem, no matter she might say. I asked her if she was planning on renovating the studio but she told me she couldn't afford it for the moment, and actually she was thinking about renting it so that she could invest in some renovations. It seemed to me she should have done it the other way round, but I chose not to talk about it. I had had enough disappointments. The second apartment wasn't really an apartment but rather a sort of dark and noisy corridor, in which it appeared impossible to live suitably, sleeping and studying. I didn't have the opportunity to see the third one, as it had just been rented to someone else by the time I arrived.

I came back to my hotel disappointed but still determined to find the perfect student place. So I spent the evening looking in other specialised rental magazines and making new appointments for the next day. Greg gave me a call to ask how I was doing. I told him about the results of my visits - though neglecting to mention the episode with Mr. Solis, of course. He was encouraging and comforting and wished me good luck for the next day. For his part, he had tried to find something too, but he had been less successful than me.

In spite of an agitated night, disturbed by all kinds of thoughts, I woke up feeling enthusiastic and full of positive energy. After all, I was in Paris, and I had a good feeling about the day ahead. This time, it was certain: it will work! Of the six appointments, surely one should be the right one. In any case, I couldn't afford to stay at the hotel for more than three or four nights, and even then, eating only sandwiches and drinking only water. That was another motivation. My dream was within reach, nothing was going to come between me and the career I dreamed of. I strode into the metro with the agile and determined attitude of someone to whom no one says no. Yet this attitude didn't serve my luck, and nothing happened as I had imagined. By the end of the day, not a single one of my new appointments succeeded with the signing of a rent agreement, nor even just an oral agreement. Very often, too many other candidates were already waiting, squeezed against one another in front of the apartment to rent, and some of them had better payment guarantees than me, and obviously more experience in the way of convincing. The bond issue was really the most difficult to solve, because my parents didn't earn enough to meet the landlord's requirements. So I returned to my hotel again, this time feeling defeated. I hadn't moved a single step forward in my hunting, my goal remaining just as elusive as when I began. When I talked to Greg on the phone, and then to my mum, about my adventure of the day, they couldn't believe it could be so complicated to rent a room in such a big city as Paris. They didn't even know what kind of advice they could give me to help. Greg suggested he could come to help me around the city. I hesitated. But a second train ticket would be expensive, without counting the costs of being in Paris itself. Everything in Paris costs a lot of money; a simple cup of coffee sitting outside could see its price going up to ten euros, about the same as ordering the dish of the day in my hometown. No, I had to do this job alone.

The next day, I thought I had reached my objective when I met the landlord of a room with toilets on the landing in a well situated quarter at a price of two hundred and seventy euros, charges included. When the man confirmed to me it was okay after having had a look at my file, I was very glad to let Greg know about this good news. At last, I would be able to go back home and to prepare for a new life. I was already memorising the daily route I would take to reach my school. Everything was alright, the room was cleaned and the neighbourhood pleasant. I had to meet the landlord again at four in front of the building to sign the contract. I allowed myself to rest a little bit in the meantime, because these two days of constant visits, bustling public transport and making appointments, with all their ups and downs, had exhausted me. At quarter to four, I was in front of the door, smiling and relaxed. By quarter past, I called the landlord to ask if he was on his way. I left a message on his answering machine. At five o'clock, I sat outside of a café, from where I could see the entry of the studio. I left three other messages, asking him to call me back or to make another appointment in case he couldn't come to see me today. I had to wait until ten thirty and twenty eight euros worth of drinks from the café for the landlord to finally find the time to call me back… the apartment wasn't available anymore. I asked for some explanation, telling him I had been waiting for him all afternoon and I was really hoping to get this studio. He answered plainly that he was sorry about that - it was simply part of the ups and downs of renting between individuals. He couldn't have done it differently as the daughter of one of his friends had called him early in the afternoon to rent the room. He couldn't have refused it - it was for a friend. He hadn't been able to let me know earlier because he had been working and wasn't available, but he said I would surely find something else.

I didn't understand how he could feel alright to change his mind like that, so offhand. I really was going from disappointment to disappointment, as if everybody had covertly agreed on discouraging me. There probably was a sign behind it - perhaps this school wasn't the right one for me, perhaps I should give up and find another subject to study in a more accessible region. It wasn't good to insist when everything was going against you. But as I was thinking about it, I remembered that it was about the dream of my life too, and that obstacles were a natural part of the effort to reach it. If I gave up at this stage, how would I be able to bear two years in this exuberant city? I had to think about it, reflecting silently about this successive wreck of failing appointments, false hopes, bad plans... However, I couldn't keep my mind clear, it was late and I was hungry. I didn't have much left in my pocket, just enough to buy a ham sandwich that I ate like a horse, sitting on a bench, while watching people eating proper meals in front of a café, just a couple of metres away from me. How could they afford to pay for this restaurant? Were they artists, business men, or rich heirs? Surely they were important people, one way or another. After having waited about another ten minutes, just in case one of the landlords would miraculously change his mind or decide out of sympathy to offer me something else, I called Greg.

- Are you alright, Laura? Have you found a place?
- No, not yet.
- Damn. I thought about you all day, though, so that you'd find something.
- It's over. I'm not going to find anything. It's impossible.
- What? Of course you're going to find something! Tomorrow, I'm sure, hun.

I hung up the phone after having promised to Greg I'd continue searching for a room the next day. Then, not in the mood to hurry back to my cheap hotel room, I decided to spend some time outside for the rest of the evening. After all, I was in one of the most beautiful cities in the world and I hadn't even had the time to visit anything yet! I walked along several famous avenues, sat on benches in a couple of squares, watching people living right there in front of me, people who definitely had a home somewhere. I envied them for having access to such a prestigious but impenetrable city. I almost wanted to go to talk to them, to ask them what they had done to find an apartment, how much they were paying for it, where they were working and how much they were earning. Then I had an idea: I could obtain this kind of information the tomorrow without doubt, by asking in a house rental agency. Even if I wasn't looking for a house with agency fees included, I was sure to find valuable help there, perhaps a few little tricks as well. I finally went back to the hotel, feeling a little bit more optimistic than a few hours before, and fell easily asleep.

Ready early the next morning, I started making my way to the quarter, looking for a house rental agency. I rapidly found three of them on a long avenue. I waited for the opening time, imagining making a discourse that corresponded to my present mind-set.

« I am looking for an affordable lease for poor people, for a poor and naïve country girl. But I still want to find something in Paris because one day, you see, I will work in the art industry and Paris is the right place for that. »

Of course, I didn't plan to introduce myself like that. But I needed to let off steam, even internally, and it made me feel good. The person welcoming me was very friendly, when I explained my situation, she confirmed me it would be difficult to find an affordable apartment in the area I wanted, and even more difficult for a clean and quiet one. She told me it was better for me to ask at social organisations specialising in student residences, but I shouldn't be in a hurry for this solution, because by the time my application would be sent and examined by a commission, I had to wait for about a month. If my family had some revenue, though, I had a much better chance to be looked after, but there was no guarantee.

I came out confused; I didn't even want to go to the other agencies. I forced myself, though, focusing hard on my objective in my mind. I received almost the same answers from the other agents, nothing available that corresponded to what I was looking for. I had to ask around at public associations or organisations, and was told to get state welfare, even before I started working. Yet, I had a budget and I wasn't asking for financial help, just a decent apartment appropriate to my wallet. I had had enough, I didn't like this imposed and uncertain commercial way, and I couldn't wait for another month to know whether I could receive any help. So what to do?

Sure, I had this other solution that would solve everything…

Mr. Solis. With him I had the assurance of a luxurious place to live, for free, in an ideal quarter, for all my student years. I thus ignored what went along with it, and the memory I now had from my visit to his home was completely different from the impression he had first left me with. I even asked myself why I had felt as offended as I did. Mr. Solis was a refined and decent person; he was just offering a generous service for what was in fact a reasonable requirement, actually. He wasn't a pervert, but a lonely man simply wanting to realise his fantasies without trouble. There wasn't any aggression in him - I could see it. For the rest, I could go along with it. I shouldn't have left him the way I did, so roughly. He didn't deserve it. He had been clear from our first contact, which certainly wouldn't be the case for a lot of other people I would meet. It made me think of him as a man full of qualities. He also had been the only one with whom I had a positive contact. That also was a good sign - the first one is always the right one, the first one always comes naturally, showing itself without or almost without effort. Suddenly, I felt anxious. But what if he had already rented it to someone else? Someone who would have understood right away the benefit and advantage of this offer. Someone cleverer than me. Of course, he already had found someone else. Quickly, I had to call him to be sure. Luckily, I still had his contact details. I feverishly dialled the number, praying it wasn't too late.

- Hello Mister Solis, it's me, Laura. I visited your apartment the other day, do you remember?
- Of course, I remember. You've run away…
- Yes, that's true. Let's say I was surprised but I've changed my mind. I am sorry about my behaviour. Have you found someone else?
- No, the rent is still available.
- Can I come to see you now?

After having picked up my things at the hotel and paid for my room, I then returned to the 8th arrondissement. I felt once again the impression I had the first time, this mix between luxury and elegance that attracted me so much, but I also had a strange and subtle feeling alongside it, something difficult to define, as if I was making an important decision for the rest of my life. I didn't know why but I felt that this decision I was taking consciously and freely would have enormous consequences for my future. It didn't stop me at all as I was making my way up the large stairs, covered by a nice reddish orange carpet. I thought about what had been my life thus far - an ordinary life, a good education, a well behaved childhood. A typical small town life for a young woman coming from a good, yet a little boring and a little too modest, family.

Mr. Solis opened his door with a satisfied smile.

- I am happy to see you again, Laura.
- Thank you, Mister.
- Please, just call me Marc, for the time being.

CHAPTER III

I took the train back to Biarritz in the evening. Just after having left Marc, I had quickly hopped onto the metro, travelling to the train station to book my ticket for half past five in the afternoon. While waiting for the train to depart, I called Greg to tell him about my flat.

- I knew you would find one today, I told you so! How lucky! Fantastic, honey!

It was of course out of question to tell him anything about the agreement I had made with the landlord – not even a detail! He wouldn't have had understood, nor approved, nor even believed what I could have explained to him. And not to mention my parents! Myself, I preferred not to think too much about these details for the moment. So, I told them I had found a room to rent in a very nice apartment which was well situated, belonging to an old man, feeling lonely after the death of his wife and desiring company. It was a unique opportunity, my rent would be very cheap and so I could easily deal with my budget.

In any case, everything was just perfect, and we - Greg and I - just had to quietly enjoy the rest of our holiday together. However, the persona I had invented for my landlord quickly forced me to repeat the lie several times over.

- I will come to see you during weekends, so that you don't exhaust yourself. Do you think your landlord will agree on that?
- I'm afraid so, he's very old, you know. We'll see.

Two weeks after, I was packing my things for Paris. My courses started in two days and I was moving in this same day at Marc's place. Secretly, I even bought some new, quality clothes, spending some of the money I was initially leaving at the side for the rent. A white shirt, raw denim jeans, a little black dress, a camel leather belt… I couldn't imagine myself walking around in a luxurious environment wearing my old jeans and cheap t-shirts. I warmly kissed my parents, who I was leaving for several months for the first time in my life, and then Greg went with me to the station, where he hugged and kissed me before I entered the train. Everybody was very caring, there to reassure me, and yet, to my big surprise, I didn't feel like I needed all this attention. I was alright, thrown into my future in what seemed the most natural way. I could have been alone, just dealing with myself for my last few days, and it wouldn't have changed my mind nor made me regret my choice.

-   I love you!
-   Me too. See you soon, Greg.
-   Are calling tonight?
-   Of course.

In the train, I thought about the next two years that looked so promising. The promise of doing the studies I had chosen, in a city where anything was possible, in order to reach my professional dream. I felt happy, and free.

When I arrived at Marc's place, a little tense after all, he was waiting for me. He had cooked, and my bedroom was ready and lit with candles. The apartment couldn't have been more welcoming. I slowly put my things away to appreciate this quiet moment, getting accustomed to the place. The atmosphere was soft but the silence was heavy. As we were having dinner, after some polite small talk, he informed me he was not going to ask anything this evening, though he would see how he felt tomorrow. I wouldn't have to stay the whole day with him, I could go for a walk and do anything I wanted as long as he was able to see me at least twice or three times a day for a couple of minutes. I spent an altogether pleasant evening with a caring, helpful and discrete host, ready to satisfy my needs. He wasn't speaking much but I could sense he wanted to have me feel comfortable. Around half past ten, I went to my bedroom and took advantage of the comfort of my own bathroom - I never had my own bathroom before! Then, after having called Greg to let him know everything was okay, I fell asleep with pleasure in clear silk sheets, dreaming of my new life.

The next morning, Marc wasn't there when I woke up. That allowed me to wander at ease around the apartment and to organise myself without inconvenience. I took my time during this first Sunday in the capital, and planned my day with just a stroll through the quarter, returning by my school to get use to the path which would soon become my daily routine. For everything else, I didn't have to care about anything because Marc had told me he would prepare each meal. Breakfast was ready, there was a relaxed atmosphere in the apartment, and the light shining through the big windows was soft thanks to some wonderful linen veils. I felt as if I were surrounded by cotton-wool. Reclining comfortably on the black leather sofa, my cup of coffee in the hand, I observed the interior of this apartment more closely. All the furniture and decoration went perfectly well together and appeared to have been chosen with care. Marc had told me that he used to work in a decoration shop and that he had inherited this apartment after the death of his parents, he was an only child and had always or almost always lived here. Now he was in charge of a furniture business, buying furniture from wholesalers and selling it to former clients of the store. The shop had closed for many financial reasons but he had negotiated the repurchase of the client's data and his business was going well. I didn't want to think about anything else than the luck I have had to take this opportunity. Just remembering the different studios I had visited - they were dirty, narrow, dark – but looking around me now…

Someone knocked on the door and I ran to open. It was Mark, holding two baskets full of fruit and vegetables.

- Morning Laura! I went to the market, and found some nice things for lunch. How do you like fish?
- I love fish. I come from the seaside, remember!
- Sure, I had forgotten. Then it's perfect.
- Why didn't you use your key?
- My hands were full, and I also thought it's better if we get use to knocking before coming in, don't you think?

I also thought it was better actually, in order to avoid embarrassing situations. This Marc really was caring and delicate. I was reminded of my clothes, a short nightgown and a top of the same colour. I had bare feet. I snuck discretely out of the lounge to change. A straight little dress and a light cotton jacket would do.

I thanked him for the breakfast, and I told him I was getting ready to take a stroll through the quarter. He reminded me I didn't have to let him know what I wanted to do – unless, of course, I really wanted to share it with him. Then, he moved to the kitchen, indicating for me to follow him for a minute. There, he put down his baskets and started to put away his shopping. He was looking at me while organising peaches and tomatoes, with an insistent look in his eyes, and I realised he was expecting a certain something from me. Yes, when we had established the terms of our oral agreement, he had been direct and clear enough about what he expected from me – he had even given me examples of words I could use. I was feeling very uncomfortable, and I felt my cheeks begin to blush. I took a breath, and the words came in a somewhat clumsy manner.

- You're worth less than nothing and you're going to prepare lunch and I want everything to be sparkling clean when I get back. You're no good for anything else…

He didn't answer, but I noticed his face changed from anticipation to satisfaction, even relief. I was so focused on repeating the words I had learned per heart, that I just had recited phrases without really putting intention in them. It didn't seem to bother Marc. As it had been discussed during our agreement, he didn't pronounce a single word and continued to put away food. So I followed his recommendations and let him do his things in the kitchen. Once in my bedroom, I sat on my bed. I couldn't believe what I had been capable of doing! That thought struck me, and I felt my cheeks burning and pressed my hands on them, watching myself in the mirror. I was red, and my eyes were wide open with surprise, with shock about what I had said. It was surreal, if I looked closely at it. Indeed, I had spoken like a machine, with words that I wasn't accustomed to using - a little like when I had tried to develop a convincing sales pitch for a summer job.

« If you're looking for a holiday rent, we can offer you a house that will satisfy both your leisure and expectations for a quiet atmosphere. Our prices are the most competitive in the region! »

I had surprised myself actually. It wasn't difficult; in fact it was almost funny – ridiculous, even. While getting dressed, lost completely in my thoughts, I was already thinking about what I would say next time, probably this evening. I would have to look in my notes, and try to learn them off by heart. I could never remember such elaborate terms off the top of my head, so I had written them down in a notebook to revisit. For the mean time, I would be speaking nicely to Marc again - according to our agreement, the rough speaking way was only reserved for certain, intimate moments. I went out without seeing him, probably still being busy cleaning the house. Outside, the weather was beautiful, and I decided to walk to the superb park, along the avenue of the apartment, that seemed to be dedicated especially to the people living in the quarter. The windows of the lounge were on this side, and I just had to look up to see them. Nothing other than windows, all alike for the whole building. It was impossible to not know who was living here or what was going on. I asked myself if Marc had had other flatmates before me, if they all fulfilled the same task, and how it might have gone. I didn't have the right to ask these questions, and he didn't want to answer them. I had to mind my own business. I already had read about these kinds of relationships before but I had never met such people. What sort of feeling did it bring? Was it possible for him to reach pleasure through it? All the same, it was astonishing to me. And what if I couldn't do it, what if all that wasn't for me? I remembered my basically conventional relationship with Greg. I was going to miss him.

This park really was a delight. It was well-kept but not too much, flowery but not too much. Huge trees grew lined along the main path, creating a sort of sheltering but spacious area under the shadow of their leaves. I walked slowly, breathing in my new environment, appreciating each step on this welcoming ground that I was now able to walk on, because I too was living there. I saw a couple of more or less elderly people and some couples with or without children who were enjoying their Sunday, too. Everybody knows Parisians run all the time. I thought I recognised the young lady I had met in the stairs for my fist visit. She smiled at me when she was passing by, still looking so elegant. It had been really been a long time since I had felt so well. I was going to get perfectly used to living in this place. I sat on a bench under the sun, next to a bed of roses, closed my eyes and kept still. I felt the warmth in my shoulders and chest, on my legs and my face. I remained so for about ten minutes. I then continued my stroll until about midday, the time at which I had planned to head back home, as Marc usually had lunch around one o'clock. When I arrived at the building, I saw he had opened all the windows facing the park, allowing the linen veils to ripple gracefully like humble and fine dancers, following the wind's gentle whispers.

- Is everything alright, Laura? Did you enjoy your walk?
- It was wonderful, an enchantment! I feel perfectly relaxed.

-   You might be hungry then. Let's eat then, shall we?

     The meal served, on the table in the sunny lounge, was delicious. Marc was a great cook - I know I certainly couldn't have done better. He had prepared everything and seemed glad to be able to share this moment. He was serving me, was looking after everything and asked nothing. I also wanted to be sure he was satisfied.

-   Marc, did I do what you expected from me?
-   Absolutely, Laura. And I know you will gain confidence with time.

     He served me a cup of coffee, inviting me to sit on the black leather sofa. We drank in silence, and that way, I was able to study his face as he was gazing out the window, illuminated by the light shining through. His eyes were deep and black, his eyebrows were cut and his hair was carefully brushed forward, his cheekbones were a little pink by the effect of the sun, his mouth was fine. He wasn't especially handsome, but he had a certain charm and emanated mystery. I couldn't figure out who he was, what he liked and even not what he was thinking by looking at him. A certain softness was coming out of his downcast eyes, though, as if he was timid yet also strong and determined at the same time. He didn't scare me at all, and in fact I was rather curious. I even admired him for his success and his direct way of speaking about extremely intimate things and of expressing his desires. His way of being didn't shock me anymore, and instead was arousing my curiosity. I had never met such a man like him before. I was use to more conventional relationships. At home, it was forbidden to disturb, to shock and to get noticed.

After the cup of coffee, my host didn't seem to expect anything more from me, so I rose and went to my room. I wanted to rest for a while before making my way to my school, preparing my clothes for the next day and checking if I had put everything in my bag. Finally, I fell asleep on my bed and woke up around three o'clock in the afternoon. It took me a couple of seconds to remember where I was, and to appreciate one more time that I had have accepted Marc's offer, in the meanwhile admiring the decorations in my white and beige room. In the bathroom, I splashed water over my forehead and neck. I didn't quite recognise myself in the mirror, my face had changed, it seemed - it had lost a little bit of its naivety.

When I came out, I bumped into Marc at the entrance. He was delicately putting the dishes away into a kitchen cabinet.

- See you soon, Laura. I would like you to spend
  a couple of minutes of your time before dinner
  tonight.
- Of course, Marc, see you later.

I now knew what these simple words meant. I
was ready, I had studied.

CHAPTER IV

When I came home, less than an hour later, the apartment was empty. I was very happy to relax and take advantage of the luxury while I was alone, so I put some music on, lit some candles and prepared a perfumed bath. After having visualised the way to school once more, I had called my parents and Greg, and now everything was ready for my first day of classes. I just had to quietly enjoy the evening and wait for Marc. I sat in the corner bathtub with massaging jets, the water was foamy and the satin sheen formed supple rainbow ripples which warped upon my skin. I watched them sliding away, uncatchable, and submerging in the water up to my chin, closed my eyes and stopped moving.

Marc arrived around half past seven. I had changed again, wearing some of the clothes I had bought before coming. A nice blue flared skirt and a white blouse embroidered with little white pearls. All the clothes put together looked fresh and light and suited the ambient warmth. When Marc saw me dressed like that, standing in the lounge, his eyes looked up and down at me but he stayed silent. He seemed to examine each fold, each stitch of fabric. Then he let his black eyes gaze into mine, and they became darker. After a couple of seconds, I drew slightly closer, without losing eye contact.

- You're a dog. You'll sleep on the ground, you piece of shit.

I found the sentence quite daring, but even so, I recited it without hesitation, having repeated it again and again during the day. For me, it didn't have any emotional or sexual value. It was sentence that didn't belong to me. I was another person as I pronounced it, playing the false role of a mistress, and carefully observing the reaction of my partner. He lifted his head slightly and this time, and could detect pleasure on his face. His lips imperceptibly opened, his eyelids went down, his nostrils quivered. Curiosity and surprise made me raise my eyebrows and my eyes opened wide. I didn't want to miss a single sensation which I effected in him with my words. I even believed to have found out that he didn't dislike the contrast between the brightness of my clothes and the crudeness of my words. I had actually already imagined the effect they would have on him while choosing these clothes, and I felt a little bit moved that my efforts had seemed to work. But he categorically warned me he couldn't bear any judgment and not even the slightest trace of doubt, which forced me to control my own emotions. With care, and in order not to spoil his delight, I slowly turned away from him and went to recline on the sofa with a magazine, not looking at him anymore. After a couple of minutes, and without transition, I heard moving in the kitchen, the noise of saucepans and the aroma of a meal.

Dinner was beautiful, as usual.

My first day at school took place as I had imagined it. I met my new classmates, my teachers, the place was pretty much alright and the program corresponded to what had been advertised. In any case, I was so happy to be there, I had dreamt so much about it - and it was all within my reach now - that I was finding the smallest corner of each painting wonderful. I just had to let myself be completely immersed in my passion: marketing and advertising of all forms of art.

After chatting with many of my classmates, I noticed they were all living at their parent's place in Paris or in the near suburbs, or they were living with one of their relatives. The few students coming from the country side were also coming from wealthier families than mine, since they were renting studios which they described as being in a very good state and close to the school. By my experience, their rent couldn't be less than three or four hundred euros.

I came back home around six o'clock after a busy day at school. We had agreed, with Marc, that I would have lunch at the university canteen, which was very close to the school, when I had courses all day. The evening was pleasant, dinner was relaxing. After dinner, just as I was going to study, my host asked me to stay for a few more seconds.

- You're learning fast, Laura, I am very satisfied. Do you feel at home in my apartment?
- Absolutely, I don't think it could be better.
- Alright, you now know my habits. I would like you to take the initiative sometimes, I would like you to surprise me.
- I'll try.

- Good. So why don't we start tonight? We'll do our things and when we'll bump into each other in a room…

I did what he expected of me. He probably had a good time.

The days followed in pretty much the same way. I left in the morning after my breakfast, without seeing Marc who generally was already out. I imagined his work was demanding enough to require his presence early in the morning, perhaps because of the time difference with his suppliers or foreign clients. I came home in the late afternoon and relaxed or studied for my courses, and then we had dinner. Each evening, we had our intimate moment - or I should say, he had his intimate moment -just after dinner, like a reward for his cooking skills, or later when the mood and spirits are roused by the night. Slowly, I had established a system to formulate sentences from certain vocabulary he had himself suggested to me, and most of all I was working on intonation, which was my weakness. I took a couple of minutes every day for a rehearsal in front of the mirror, like an actress. I played my role for a few seconds then I went back to my daily activities, as if nothing had happened. I never thought whether what I was doing was right or wrong, if it was good or bad. It only concerned Marc and me, and, well, as long as we were disturbing nobody… I regularly called Greg and my parents, and chatted about my courses, my classmates, my teachers. Every time they asked questions about my landlord I remained vague, explaining to them that an old man doesn't move a lot and that the quiet environment suited me very well for my studies.

After two weeks, I decided to travel back to Biarritz for the weekend. I missed Greg and my family too, and I wanted to smell the sea again. Marc reminded me I could do what I wanted as long as I was fulfilling my part of the agreement when I was there. He wished me a nice stay and said he would wait for me on Sunday evening and dinner would be ready when I arrived.

Seeing my family was a real pleasure. My parents prepared my favourite meals, and Greg offered me a present: a fine white golden necklace. I completely forgot my Parisian life for a weekend. I found myself back home, having been away so briefly, back in my neighbourhood, in my city, with my friends. My fiancé was very in love and our intimate moments were a complete delight. However, time flew by and already it was time to leave. Greg went with me to the station early on

Sunday afternoon, and this separation new caused tears for both of us. I sat in the train, waving my hand from behind the window, and then as the train got going I immersed myself in a book specialised in interior decoration which I had borrowed from Marc's book case. He had suggested it to me because there was an article talking about him and his work in it. But I couldn't concentrate on reading. Something was disturbing me. I tried to close my eyes and weird images unwillingly appeared in my mind. I was seeing Marc in all kinds of submissive positions looking shameful to the point of being grotesque. All that was disturbing me but I couldn't stop these creations of my own imagination. How far would he compel me to go? For the moment, we hadn't gone beyond the level of words, a few seconds of humiliation, but if he wanted to go further, what kind of solution would I find in that case? I couldn't see myself doing more, in any case, not while remaining a healthy step back. The contrast between my family environment, my upbringing and Greg's serious demeanour with my landlord's secret and perverted life were shocking. It felt like a warning bell. Could it be that right and wrong really do exist in that situation and that I had to make a decision? And then, what I was doing in exchange for certain advantages, wasn't it basically prostitution? Of course, I had had the intuition from my first contact with Marc but unconsciously or not,

I immediately hadn't considered this fact further because I was focusing on my professional goal, and had forgotten my suspicion. I might have been wrong, since it wasn't common, actually. And even though I certainly hadn't enjoyed belittling Marc, nor had I seen any problem in doing it. I hadn't really felt disturbed about it. So why did all these thoughts arise at a time like this, suddenly, giving me doubts?

My cellphone rang, it was Marc. I got up to go into the train's corridor.

- Laura ? Are you on your way ? I wanted to know when you're going to be there, for the gratin.

When I saw him, a little bit later, my doubts had disappeared. Everything I had found shocking just before didn't seem serious anymore, at Marc's place, in Paris. Was it the effect of this incredible city or my host's charisma? Tired of thinking about all that, I chose the simplest way and the solution which was the most convenient for me: we had a relation based on trust and common interests, so there was nothing else to say.

Days passed by, evening after evening with Marc. I gained more confidence, learned to introduce pauses, moments of suspense between my sentences, and different tones that seemed to add to the desired effect. I had noticed that some questions, if they were asked at the right time – for example, *You know that you don't deserve to eat at the table, you must lick your food off the floor, you know that, don't you?* - were bringing him more pleasure if I pronounced them very slowly, close to him, insisting hard on certain words like *lick*, or *on the ground*, and watching him going down.

I didn't feel anything particular in those moments, except for the satisfaction of meeting my part of the agreement. I knew that after around ten minutes, we would just go about our own business in our almost normal lives. This role might seem strange to play for a couple of minutes before going back to our busy life, but we were doing it without effort, actually. We sometimes talked a little more about his job and his favourite topic, decoration, in which I became more and more interested myself, because it represented an artistic field quite like sculpture, painting or writing... However, we never talked about his private life, about his life outside of the apartment and at work. Yet I knew he often had to go out and I wasn't sure if it always was for professional matters. But he avoided every personal discussion and always changed the topic when I tried to talk about it. Nobody came to his place and I almost never met anybody in the building, except for the young woman I had seen the first time, who often arrived at the time as me. She would smile at me, answer my greeting and return to her home on the lower floor. When my classmates suggested to me to go out to the theatre or to the cinema or to come to visit them, I simply called Marc who took no offence at eating alone. He always was of the same mood, always caring about my well-being. Over the days and weeks, my interventions began to come more intuitively. I almost didn't have to prepare my sentences anymore. I knew when I had to do please him - his eyes were enough to make me understand what he expected from me, at which intensity, and for how long…

In November, as I hadn't returned to Biarritz for two months, Greg suggested spending a weekend with me in Paris. I talked to Marc about his idea.

- My boyfriend would like to come and see me. Is it going to disturb you, Marc?
- Let's say that we, as an exception, could organise his visit. In two weeks I have to go abroad for work. Tell him to come on that weekend. Both of you will be able to enjoy the apartment. Would that be okay for you?

I thanked Marc for his offer. I was relieved he was going to be away during Greg's visit because I was afraid Greg would notice our special complicity in one way or another. And on top of that, I had told him that Marc was an old man… So with Marc away, we would be able to completely enjoy being with each other in this wonderful environment. I couldn't wait to show Greg my quarter, the best spots around Paris I had discovered and the apartment where I had the chance to live. I was waiting for his visit with impatience and Marc noticed it.

- You're really in love, aren't you?
- Yes, that's right! We'll live together as soon as I graduate.

When I saw Greg coming out of the train on Friday evening, I ran into his arms. I had been so impatient to see him, to fall asleep with him. I had prepared a sort of activity plan I had thought about for the weekend, and first of all, I had organised a romantic dinner at the apartment which I had decorated with candles and flowers. I wanted him to spend a wonderful weekend because I wasn't sure if we could do it again, and then, it made me feel good too, to act once more as a normal intimate couple and to take a break from my *relation* with Marc.

Greg was amazed by the apartment he found very nice and luxurious. He couldn't believe the luck I had to live there.

- It's extraordinary that you have found this old man!
- Yes, well … He isn't really that old.

He found that as an old man, his apartment was pretty modern and even a little bit avant-garde in some places. It should be mentioned that Marc was collecting contemporary photography, especially nudes, and he didn't dislike a kitsch object here and there to break the extreme bareness of some of the contemporary furniture. The whole look was very stylish and suited him perfectly, but of course, didn't correspond to the idea Greg had of my landlord according to what I had told him in very few details. As we were walking by Marc's bedroom, commenting the decoration, Greg couldn't resist opening his door to have a look in the inside. I, myself, had never dared to cross this limit, or even felt like it. Embarrassed, I was ready to ask him to close the door, when he suddenly naively asked:

- Oh, is there a dog here?
- No. Why do you ask that?
- Look, a long dog leash, there, on the chest of drawers, near the bed. Very nice bedroom, but a little bit too dark for me.

Feeling embarrassed by Greg's question, and also by the presence of this object, I immediately pulled his arm back and quickly closed the bedroom's door before he decided to investigate. Asking him if he was hungry to divert his attention, I took him to the lounge where the table was ready set and ready for dinner and was waiting for us.

The rest of the weekend went well. We could enjoy everything the city had to offer in the best conditions. I took him to see the main monuments, a play at the theatre and even to my school, so that he can see it with his own eyes. He never stopped repeating that I was lucky, that he would have loved to share all that with me. He had no more questions or thoughts about my landlord, and seemed to have forgotten the dog leash episode. I was wondering if this accessory really was meant to be used for what I imagined. Could it be that Marc used it during his intimate games? Was he soon going to ask me to use it? I wouldn't be capable of doing that. Our agreement was based on words only, and that was hard enough, and I hoped to remain on this simple agreement. Did I have to make the first move and talk to him about it? It was tricky because he could take the opportunity to bring forward his request to take things further, if that was what he wished for. It also meant that I had entered into his room and destroyed the trust he had placed in me.

On Sunday evening, I went with Greg to the station, and then back to the empty apartment. I felt a twinge of sadness while turning the latch to close the door. I had spent a wonderful weekend with my boyfriend, and yet, I was feeling down, a kind of weariness. I had lied to him about my landlord and about the relationship I was having with him, even though these questions were actually related to a sexual service and Greg was my fiancé. There was something shameful in there, and I knew this realisation was probably related to the discovery of this dog leash, too.

Pulled by a wild curiosity, I slowly made my way to Marc's bedroom.

CHAPTER V

I came into the room without switching the light on, preferring instead to let my eyes get used to the dark. Perhaps was I afraid of what I would discover. The leash was sitting there conspicuously on the mahogany chest of drawers. As I moved closer, I could better distinguish the sharp nails on the dark piece of leather. I didn't touch the object, instead just observing it with curiosity. Marc had never spoken about a dog before and never mentioned any interest for animals. So why this dog leash then? The rest of the bedroom was in perfect order, exactly as he liked leaving his apartment when he was going out. I opened half of the first furniture's drawer. My hand was doing the movement, following my curiosity, while my reason was telling the opposite. I was breathing faster - I knew I would probably regret this move. What I saw confirmed my worries; heaps of straps, rough ropes and leather fabrics matched with metal, all piled up in the overfilled drawer. It looked like stock of industrial materials or marine equipment, according to the references which first popped into my mind. Then I looked closer and opened the drawer wider. I pulled out the first leather strap that fell into my hand. It just kept on coming I had to pull myself back a little to be able to stretch out its full length. There were actually two straps about two meters long that were bound together by a metal ring on one end and a rivet on the other. There were several snap fasteners towards the last centimetres of it, as if they could be put together. How would he use this object? I didn't have clue about it. I continued my investigation and so took out, one after the other, all the elements of this incredible gothic chaos. I recognized among so many impossible to identify objects a piece of underwear and a cat-o'-nine tails - well, that's what I thought at least. Then I put everything on the ground and sat on the bed to look over all the equipment. I might have looked like someone having discovered after many years that his good dog was in fact a bitch in heat.

What to do now? Put everything back in place and act as if nothing happened? Or talk to Marc about it and take the risk of losing my so comfortable life? He should be back within two days, so I decided to give me time to reflect upon it and go back to my studies. I had tonnes of things to prepare for the weekly courses ahead and only the evenings to do it. This would help me focus and avoid having it all stuck in my mind. Feeling puzzled, I took my exercise books, sat at a desk Marc had prepared for me and tried to immerse myself in art history. Amongst other things, I had plenty of research to do online. Connecting took a couple of seconds, enough to allow my thoughts to leave the Renaissance and its painters. In the search bar, I wrote *submissive relations*. The results suggested to me *Domination and submission*.

"Physical contact isn't necessary (...). In some other cases, it can be intensively physical. (...) A lot of submissive wear a "collar" to show their status and engagement."

(...)

« (...) a study has shown (...) people who play this kind of games could be mentally healthier than those having a more classical sexuality. More extravert, more open to new experiences, less neurotic, these people also have obtained lower scores than the general public about sensitivity towards being rejected, a higher level of well-being and have expressed a stronger feeling of affection in their relationships. »

The articles were in particular about relations based on the search for intense sensations, with created codes between the participants to keep limits. There were a lot of little practical details and some of them seemed incredible. And yet, I realised that even if I wasn't interested at all, I understood what the fans were looking for. It wasn't about love, nor even about hate, but about the search for the strongest pleasure possible through transgression. What disturbed me, after having seen Marc's equipment, was that his relations wouldn't be limited to words, as I had thought they would be, because a lot of these objects clearly were designed to cause physical pain, or in any case to remind you of it.

Absorbed in my reading, I didn't notice the time passing by. When I realised I hadn't yet started my study, it was already three o'clock in the morning. Exhausted, I fell asleep on the sofa without having been capable of writing a thing. A couple of hours after, I woke up too late to go to class. I ate a little bit, had a shower, then continued with my research on the Internet until the evening. At seven in the evening, at last, I decided to work on my studies, which I finally finished around midnight. Marc was meant to come back the next evening, and from now on, I knew more about the nature of his practices. I didn't judge him but I was sure I couldn't satisfy him with physical demands if he asked me. I had to talk to him about that because I felt the question wouldn't easily leave me and could end up disturbing my studies. It was out of question for me to take this risk.

Actually, I wasn't happy about him now. Was there really a way to know if he only had limited his requests in order not to scare me and to push me to accept his agreement? And if he suddenly felt like putting it into action, all of a sudden, giving in to an impulsion one evening, when I would have no way to escape, and nobody to hear my scream? I already had read this kind of story in the newspapers and this could turn out to be nightmare. It was a little bit ridiculous because Marc never put himself in a dominating position, and there was no reason to think he would suddenly reverse the roles... He didn't seem to have anticipated at all the damages he could cause in my life, when inviting me into his own intimate life. That was very selfish of him.

Harassed by these thoughts, causing me all sorts of doubts about my landlord, and finally about myself, I ended up falling asleep, exhausted but determined to keep control over the situation. He wouldn't get what he wanted from me.

The next day was a hard one during which I tried to catch up on my day off, asking my classmates for help. They thought I was looking preoccupied and were worried about my behaviour.

When I came back to the apartment, it was more than half past seven. Marc was there. He greeted me with a big smile and spontaneously asked me if I had spent a good weekend with my fiancé.

- Great, Marc. Thank you very much for having let us enjoy the apartment. My boyfriend really liked the way it's decorated and thinks I'm very lucky.

- Are you?

- I don't know. What do you think?

- I think I am the one being lucky. For having found you.

- Did you find me or did you look for me?

- Both I think.

- And I bring you what you're expecting?

- Well … yes. I think I already told you that.

- It was before, is it still true?

- What's the matter, Laura? You seem strange. Did something happen with your boyfriend?

- No, it's not that. But I wanted to ask you a question. What do people do with a dog leash?

- What do you mean?

- A dog leash. A leather dog leash with nails.

- Oh, I understand. You've been in my bedroom, haven't you?

- That's true, I know I shouldn't have. But recognise that such an object could only arouse my curiosity.

- I hope so. Honestly, I let it there conspicuously on purpose. I wanted to know if you were curious, and to know your reaction too.

- Really? So, what then?

- So I'm satisfied. You're curious, and you're honest. So we broke the ice which remained between us, don't you think?

- I'm not quite sure I follow. What do you expect from me?

- Nothing more, Laura. You're perfect and I hope you'll stay.

- You're not going to ask anything else?

- No, nothing more. Don't worry. I told you, this object was designated to get closer us to each other, nothing more. Come, I've prepared dinner.

I followed him without saying anything, stunned. How was it possible he anticipated my behaviour that easily? I felt stupid and guilty, but at the same time, Marc fascinated me, even if someone else could objectively have described his attitude as that of a manipulator. We were now sitting comfortably one in front of the other, enjoying the meal he had carefully prepared as always. However, something had changed, he was right, a conventional barrier had fallen, and I felt much closer to him than before. That night, we were almost a real couple. When, after dinner, he insistently looked at me, I exactly knew what I had to say.

The first days following the evening were idyllic. I was so relieved to be able to stay at Marc's place I could have hugged all my classmates, and even everybody I met. Having been able to speak freely about what troubled me made me feel safe and encouraged me to thank my host for his understanding. I was satisfying him very much, all without crossing my reasonable verbal limits. Feeling more confident now, thanks to my research and my reading, I better sensed what he wanted without needing him to clearly express it, and I found the rights words at the right time. I was pretty proud of myself, as if I was daily practicing a subtle and fine art, like a sort of dominating geisha. Marc seemed to enjoy the effort and really didn't ask for more. He was living his life like before, disappearing sometimes in the evening and only reappearing the next day, always smiling and reassuring.

This enthusiasm spread to my studies too. I was taking them just as seriously as my role of intimate "partner". My teachers congratulated me, my classmates came to me for advice, and it was as if I was carried by a wave of success and respect. I didn't even realise the time that had passed by, and I hadn't returned to Biarritz for more than a month. When Greg called me, I always postponed, saying that I had to study, my landlord needed me, the school was organising a special weekend, I was sick... All of that was true, although I could have said no to some invitations or suggestions which I had nevertheless accepted. I didn't miss my boyfriend because I was so absorbed in my activities and I didn't have any free time. However, when I counted the number of days from my last visit to my parents and my boyfriend until now, I realised it actually was time to go back and see them. Especially with Christmas coming, it was inconceivable to spend the holidays away from my family. It was obvious for everybody that I would come back for this occasion, and even if my parents seemed relaxed on the phone, they were probably anxious without daring to let me know. My poor parents, who had never been to Paris, never been beyond Bordeaux… They couldn't imagine the life I was having here.

So I took the train to Biarritz on a Friday afternoon, after having wished Marc happy holidays and letting him know about my return time the following Sunday evening, on Christmas Day. I didn't plan to stay longer down in Biarritz because I and my classmates had class preparations to work in a team. Marc was keen on coming to pick me up at the station this time, so I wouldn't have to worry about anything. The trip was pleasant, quiet and relaxing, and I found Greg waiting as I came out of the train, late in the evening. I had confirmed to my parents we would see them the next day for lunch, they seemed very happy about it.

- You look gorgeous, honey! You look like you're coming back from holidays!

- It's almost that. I have the impression of being on holiday though I'm studying twelve to fourteen hours a day!

- Come, let's go, I really want to listen to all that in person. I've had enough of only speaking to you over the phone.

Greg seemed glad to see me and had planned a lot of things to do but for this Friday evening, he just wanted us to be alone together. So he had asked his parents to let us the house for the night. They had accepted and took the opportunity to visit a close cousin until the next day. Greg offered me a very nice silk scarf with soft colours. I had completely forgotten to buy him something, and I was very embarrassed but he reassured me it wasn't important.

- Did you miss me?
- A lot.

He was very gentle, very tender, he took my clothes off with care and wrapped me between of his arms. When he started caressing my face, I felt something strange, a sort of unease, as if this extreme softness irritated me. His hands seemed too limp, his movements too slow, his care for satisfying me too much. Yet, Greg had always been like this with me. I recognized his movements, the way he looked at me, but I didn't want them at all tonight.

- Sorry. I'm really tired.

- Oh! I'm sorry. Come, in that case, let's go to sleep. That's alright.

We spent the next day with my parents, who never stopped asking questions about my life in Paris, my landlord, my studies. I reassured them, and promised to invite them for a visit of the city as soon as possible. They were extremely happy, everything was going well but I felt embarrassed to have rejected Greg after so much time away from one another. It might have been because of that, because of the passing time, which had made me lose the feeling of being used to having his body against mine. It would come back.

However, in the evening, as we both were lying in my childhood bed at my parent's place after Christmas Eve meal, I rejected him again, saying I was feeling uneasy and I was afraid someone would hear us.

- What's the matter, Laura? Is there a problem?

- No, not at all. It's just because it has been so long. I don't know, I need a little bit of time.

- But you're going away tomorrow! Come, come to me.

So I forced myself to respond to his caresses but only with a certain reserve, but Greg didn't seem to notice it. He didn't say anything else, didn't complain, even if I never had been so passive, so tense and distant during sex. I would almost have cried to realise how much I didn't want him.

The next day, he still didn't dare to speak about my behaviour, and I took the train back to Paris with this unfulfilling impression. I, myself, didn't know what to say, and during the way back, I thought about this failed visit, telling myself it was the first time I behaved like that with Greg. Before, if I would have wanted to say no, it always was for a good reason and it never had any consequences on our relationship. This time, I felt something was going wrong but I really didn't know what. I tried to analyse what I had felt in his arms - it wasn't disgust or fear, rather it was a kind of irritation. But why? Greg hadn't changed, I didn't think so.

Marc was waiting for me on the platform in Paris as he had said, his thin figure wrapped with his overcoat over a perfectly well cut suit and a white blouse without tie, as usual. He even had a bunch of flowers in his hands, and a wonderful book of art photography, which he offered me as we greeted each other.

- I'm happy to see you again, Laura.

- Thanks Marc, you shouldn't have.

I was pleased with so much care and attention, I had to admit it. I was the woman with the double life, like in the movies, and it didn't scare me at all - on the contrary, it stimulated me. We came back without speaking and Marc left after dinner, explaining he had to go out. I took the opportunity to go to bed early because I had class the next day and I really wanted to continue working hard in my studies. Without this trouble with Greg, my life would have been perfect. But yet... the memory of the time spent in his arms, waiting for the end... It was painful. I called him straight away the next day to apologise and to see whether he still had bad feelings. But distance doesn't help with confidence, and on the phone we didn't succeed in washing away the uneasy feeling that had appeared. He promised me to call more regularly though, and to come to

visit me soon. I had the impression he was saying
that to warn me and to deal with his own fears.

73

CHAPTER VI

Days passed by, full of classes and study, and dinners and more with Marc. There were no questions, no clashes; we were like the world's best friends, caring for each other in our own special way, chores for him, and "play" for me. Normally always very serious, I began to get comfortable and allowed myself to improvise a little and try new things, which one day made us have a fit of the giggles, destroying all sexual excitement. A wholly involuntary slip made me say *you deserve to be stomped upon by my crap mate's stilettos*, instead of *classmate's stilettos*...

Sometimes, on Sunday, we went walking together in the park by the apartment. It was Marc who had suggested it to me, and to my big surprise, I particularly appreciated these moments, when we were showing a little bit of our complicity - more or less voluntarily. I imagined someone who knew him very well might cross paths with us on our walk, and ask themselves what kind of relationship Marc and me might have together. I was having fun, and it was making the walk juicier. We weren't talking much, only about work and art, at least most of the time, but we liked looking at trees and plants, trying to guess their name, or sometimes we would simply sit on a bench and people-watch. On occasion we would bump into the young neighbour from the floor below us, who always greeted us with the utmost politeness and continued walking. Marc always said she didn't look very interesting, though I didn't agree with him. I, myself, still didn't know anybody in our quarter but it was true I didn't have a lot of time outside of my daily activities and my private time with Marc. He, himself, seemed to know all the salespeople, and would wave when passing in front of their shops. I admired him for living his life fully, not only on the professional level but also on a personal, sexual level. I still didn't know if he had any other *playing* partners than me, or if he was using his *special* accessories on occasion - I didn't know anything of it. And this mystery all around him was making him as sublime as he was inaccessible. I only had certain moments, here and there, when he let me take control over him. So with whom did he really share his life?

He didn't have his parents anymore but perhaps he had brothers and sisters, perhaps a boyfriend or a girlfriend somewhere, or had he already have been married? I couldn't believe he was completely alone, even if I could see for myself he was someone who needed a lot of freedom, a lot of independence in his life. He liked me because I left from morning to evening and because I studied after dinner until late at night. We didn't owe anything to one other. In the end, he was the one who had control over me, since he knew everything about my simple life whereas I didn't know anything of his, and even when he allowed me to take control, he was actually the one deciding when and for how long. Who, then, was really in control?

Then, one day, just as he had finished setting the table, which he brightened with candles and flowers, he suggested to me that I sit down, and offered me a glass of wine.

- Laura, would you like to go out with me on Saturday evening? We could go to see a show and have dinner in a restaurant. You are my guest, of course.

- I don't know if that's a good idea, Marc. We
  have a, well, professional relationship,
  remember.
- Exactly - I consider it to be part of our
  agreement. I ask you to come with me for one
  evening, if you like.
- Don't you have anybody else to go with?
- No, nobody for this Saturday, only you.
- I'll think about it.

This apparently harmless offer was arousing
my curiosity. If now we were going to go out
together, people who knew Marc really could think
we were more than just simple flatmates. I was
surprised he wasn't embarrassed about it, as he
obviously relished mystery. But after all, there
wouldn't be any consequences for me, and I really
wanted to discover places where my classmates
surely didn't go to. Probably, they were very chic
and very expensive places, the sort of places where I
wouldn't be able to afford to pay for myself for a
long time yet. After having thought about it, I
decided I was up for it.

The evening was planned for the coming
weekend, in three days, and already I was looking
forward to it. Despite my excitement, I didn't speak
to either Greg or my parents about it during our

phone calls. Nor did I say a word about it to my classmates. Only the day before did I realise I didn't really have anything suitable to wear - not even one evening dress, not even any smart looking blouse – as I imagined, anyway. I was actually wondering if I was able to fit in at all, in an environment that was surely ten thousand miles away from the standards of my country town. For I, a mere country girl still fresh in Paris, didn't have the refined manners or slightly contemptuous detachment of a true Parisian. It was said there were very few true Parisians, but anyway, some had certainly been living here for a long time, and sometimes I got the feeling my origins were as obvious as a goat in a wolf pack. The way I carried myself, my way of naively smiling, of looking directly, how I wore my clothes… How, then, should I behave for the coming evening? What if we met Marc's acquaintances? I shared my doubts with him.

- Come on, Laura, we're not at the British Court, and I'm not taking you to meet important celebrities! Relax, don't worry. As for your clothes, I'll choose something for you. You will wear the nice black dress I saw you wearing one evening last week. It'll be perfect!
- Isn't that dress a bit close-fitting?

- Yes, that's the one! It's perfect for going out in the evening! You're not a nun, are you?

I found the tone a little bit out of place, but I liked when Marc was in a good mood. He was more familiar with me, and thus a little closer.

The next evening, I came home a bit earlier than usual, deciding to take full advantage of the evening, which appeared to be full of surprises. Marc, always used to keeping an air of mystery, hadn't let slip a single detail about the restaurant where we were going to eat, nor about the show. He only had told me it would be exceptional. So I started to prepare myself with care, waiting for him to come. It was five o'clock and we wouldn't be leaving until about half past seven, so I had a plenty of time to put make up on and to pay careful attention to every little detail of my appearance. As he had reassured me about my ability to fit in with the group, I wanted to impress him and show him what a little country town girl was capable of. Besides the black dress he had recommended me, I chose a tiny light brown leather belt and shoes with slight heels. I did my make-up a little more pronounced than usual, picked out a little red bag, and put my hair in a loose bun, which gave a lot of volume to the whole look. My hair had grown a lot these last months, and I hadn't taken the time to trim the ends. Marc had already told me he liked its golden bronze colour a lot - it couldn't have been anyone other than an interior decorator to use such words to describe colours. Golden brown, vermilion, steel blue… he knew all the nuances and made poetry out of simple colours. Around seven o'clock, just as I finished polishing my nails, he knocked on the door. When he saw me, his eyes grew wider.

- You look superb, Laura.
- Thanks, Marc.
- We'll be leaving within three quarters of an hour, just the time I need to get dressed up to the same level as you.

As we sat in his car, I asked him again if he could tell me more about the show we were going to watch. To my surprise, he answered the show would be for the second part of the evening, and we were going to have dinner first. I had imagined the contrary, for whatever reason, but in any case, I was pretty hungry and was happy to let him organise everything. Dinner was fantastic. Marc had reserved a table in a very famous restaurant, with a simple and quiet atmosphere, which served very fine cuisine. He explained to me that he himself had had done the decoration some months ago, though he still hadn't eaten there, but he knew the both the chef as well as the landlord, who were also his privileged clients. Our table was in a quiet and discreet corner with a view towards the entrance, so that we could look at the people coming in and comment on their look. Marc said he knew several people sitting there who couldn't see us from where they were eating. There were clients, associates, and work partners. When dessert came, a popular specialty from this restaurant, he wrapped my eyes with a scarf and made me guess all the flavours composing the dessert. I was under his spell. When we stood up to leave the restaurant, he greeted a couple sitting a few tables away from ours and presented me as a friend. He let me know it was a famous art dealer - I was very impressed. We went out into the street, laughing like two friends enjoying a good evening and taking advantage of life's pleasures. I felt better and better with him and I even found we were starting to form a nice couple. When we arrived close to the car, a few streets away, Marc reminded me the evening wasn't over yet and he was taking me now to a place he really liked. I was looking forward to finding out where he spent some of his mysterious evenings – sometimes even whole nights – when he was away from home. I let him organise everything, trusting him completely and without resistance. The car stopped in a very busy street and Marc parked his car in a little private parking lot, thanks to an access card. He opened the door for me and helped me out, and then he took my arm and led me to a building which looked almost exactly like a nightclub, though it had a very discreet look, so that it was impossible to guess there could be any quality show in this kind of place. The guard standing in front of the entry greeted my private guide with respect.

- Good evening Monsieur Solis.
- Good evening François.

The entrance hall in which we came in was very dark and despite the night which had crept upon the streets outside, I needed some time to get my eyes used to the dim, softly-coloured lights which revealed only form and shadow. I thought we were in one of those numerous fashion clubs and we were going to watch a strip-tease show or some traditional stylish Parisian dance. I had never put a foot in this kind of place - it was a first for me. We left our stuff at the cloakroom and someone took us without a word to a small, sort of half isolated lounge with two tables and comfortable sofas. In the half-light I could only guess the presence of other people between the lounges and, as I imagined, in the same lounge as ours. I heard the delicate notes of languorous music playing quietly, travelling through these soft spaces, and caught the scent of delicate perfumes infusing the atmosphere.

- Isn't it nightclub? It seems like some sort of nightclub.
- Yes, you could say that, Laura. You'll see, relax and let's order some drinks.

We already had drunk quite a lot at the restaurant and I would have been satisfied with just a juice but Marc insisted on ordering a bottle of champagne.

- Are we celebrating something?
- Perhaps - I still don't know. We'll decide later.

More mystery. I would really never be able to solve all the secrets of my evening partner's personality. I guessed that something particular was planned. However, Marc had spoken about a show - where could that show take place? Right inside our lounge? Or in that room with golden lights a little bit further along, which I could see now that my eyes were used to the dark?

Champagne was served and Marc raised his glass towards me.

- To us, dear Laura!

I found he had been particularly attentive to me since he had made the invitation for this evening. I was very glad about it but at the same time, I couldn't help but detect a desire to get us closer and that made me feel unsure about his real intentions. Did he want to tell me something serious, to speak about something important? I hadn't the faintest idea. Suddenly I heard sounds, noises came from the golden room, people were moving, and seemed to be forming an audience. I understood the show was getting started. I was quite relieved because it meant there was a show for all the clients and not just for the two of us, which would have made me feel very uncomfortable. I questioned Marc with my eyes but he didn't answer, instead just smiling impishly, making me understand I had to be patient. After about ten minutes, a lot of people, coming from I don't know where, were gathering in the room and started to make a circle around the centre. Marc stood up and offered his hand, asking me to follow him. It was the first time he was taking my hand and I felt deeply moved by that. I liked the contact of my hand with his palm, even if it seemed a bit sudden. We joined the group which now circled all around the room. Marc made me stop in a spot where we could see the whole scene and stood behind me. He was taller than me and I felt his breath on my neck, which really had me completely stunned. I gazed at the decoration as louder and more rhythmical music began to play, creating a dramatically different atmosphere. There, there was a kind of huge black leather armchair, a long and narrow table, two stools and a bunch of accessories which usually would be found in a kitchen. All this made me think of a theatre piece. But I didn't have time to ask myself other questions. Three people appeared in the middle, were dressed in leather and metal. There were two women and a man, and they went about here and there, dancing and looking towards the attentive spectators, who were all were standing very close to the actors, so close they could touch them without moving. I understood very quickly. There were no preliminaries, no useless explanations. The scene was obscene and explicit. It lasted for a few minutes – or perhaps half an hour. I couldn't tell - I was horrified, though I didn't dare to move, with the tension was so heavy in the group. I felt Marc still there behind me, very close, but I didn't turn around because I felt so embarrassed. I didn't dare to look towards anyone else's eyes, and I knew my young age was catching the attention in this kind of place. I waited for the end, and then took advantage of some people's movements to quickly escape out of the circle. I had seen enough, I wanted to go away.

I ran into the entrance hall where I immediately asked for my stuff, bumped into a man asking me if I was single, though I responded only with a swear word, and then ran out of the building without bothering to wait for my partner who didn't come out before I could hail a taxi. Marc then arrived just behind me, calling me from the other side of the street. I didn't answer. In the taxi, after having given the address of the apartment, I took a deep breath, not only because I was puffed, but also to get the memory of the show out of my head. How could Marc dare to take me to this kind of place? What was he thinking about? Did he think I would like that, those obscene puppets that were beating and humiliating each other in the most disgusting ways? Did he think I would fall into his arms and we would have sex tonight in his well-equipped bedroom? Or did he think he could then bring me along to such evenings where I was sure he sometimes acted himself too? What a delusion! I was so happy about the idea that our relationship would evolve towards if not love then at least feelings of mutual esteem. But it wasn't his objective at all, what he wanted was a partner for his extreme sexual games. He wanted to take me to places like that to do degrading things like we just saw! Who did he think he was? I may not be a nun but I was neither immoral nor a pervert. He had gone too far and I would tell him frankly as soon as he stepped into the apartment, even if this time it would mean our separation. My studies didn't cost that much. I was so angry that I didn't take my clothes off and slumped into an armchair close to the door, deciding to throw everything at him when he arrived.

After about ten minutes of waiting, pondering, and then dozing, I fell asleep right there without noticing.

CHAPTER VII

I was woken both the sun and a slight headache. I put my hands on my forehead as if to bring relief and help open my eyes. A glance at the clock by the entrance told me it was ten o'clock. With difficulty, having sore muscles and feeling tense, I rose out of the armchair, and I went to the door of Marc's bedroom, which I opened without knocking. The bed hadn't been used and nobody was to be found, so Marc hadn't come back. I took a step back to look at myself in the mirror in the hallway, judging the damages after this nightmarish night. Where had the fresh young woman from yesterday gone, who before the same mirror had so carefully put up her long hair together on the top of her head? My bun was now half undone, my tights were laddered, my makeup had run, I didn't recognise myself. Some months ago I had a fiancé, a normal family, a quiet student life and projects to occupy myself. Today I looked like a poor girl lost in a city and environment too big, too sophisticated and especially too dangerous for her. I had to stop here, go back to Greg if it wasn't too late and above all, get out of this place. Panicking, I quickly took my clothes off, ran into the shower and scrubbed myself violently with a massage glove. I had the feeling of being dirty, to have done something that had tainted me. I wanted to make this feeling disappear, so that nobody could ever guess what I had seen, the place I had been, and who with. I had to wash all that away from my memory, and I had to start with my skin because the smells and perfumes were still surrounding me. I threw the dress, the tights and the belt away - everything should disappear! Then, after having put the most ordinary clothes on, I started emptying my drawers and gathering my stuff on the bed ready for packing. Quick! I would go to a hotel to begin with, then I would find a youth hostel or a home of any kind or a simple bedroom - it would be enough to finish my studies. This was what I should have done from my arrival in Paris. What a crazy thing to have wanted to enjoy such luxury that couldn't have possibly been for free! I had behaved like an idiot.

I was putting the last of my clothes into my suitcase when I heard a knock at the door. After hesitating a moment, I went to open it. It was Marc. He had changed too - I don't know where - and he had a disappointed look on his face.

- Laura, why did you run away like that? Look, nobody was going to eat you! I thought you were an adult!
- Well, you've made a mistake. And I find you disgusting, I'm leaving, my bags are ready.
- What? No, come on, don't leave. I promise you I won't disturb you again.
- Now you're the one taking me for a kid. You didn't "disturb" me, you've assaulted me!
- I didn't touch you. And that wasn't my intention.
- Why did you take me to such a place then?
- I thought I could show you the trust I had placed in you like that. You're the only one around me with whom I can share this.
- Around you? Who else? There's nobody with you or at your place. And do you think that because I make an effort to answer to your demands that it means I am enjoying this kind of situation? Not at all! If I'm pleasing you, it's only to have a roof above my head - that's all. But I'll find another one, and it'll cost me less.

- You're very harsh, Laura. But, I will make sure you again can enjoy your stay here. And I promise you not to bring you along to these kinds of evenings anymore. Trust me and you won't regret it. If you want, you can come with me to my workplace when you don't have class. I'll introduce you to the people I deal with and you'll see that my professional life is extremely normal. If nobody comes here, it's because you're the only one I'm pleased to have in my private sphere. Please, I ask you to forgive me.

Incredulously, suitcases in hands, I watched him begging me to stay. The scene looked exactly like some tragic movie, and I could have decided not to participate in the scenario, yet I felt flattered and touched by Marc's concern. He was playing with my feelings and I hadn't imagined he would insist so much to convince me to stay and put so much effort into persuading me he had good intentions. He didn't want to hurt me, I was sure of that. His clumsiness was touching, and I thought I understood him better for it: he sometimes showed himself to be very caring, and sometimes didn't fully realise what he was doing, following his desires without thinking about it. I had to admit this also was a part I liked in him, his way of living his preferences without going by normal expectations. Because of that, he could behave awfully as well as irresistibly, and he really had a way to turn me upside down, me and my resolutions.

- I'll think about it.
- Thanks, Laura.
- I don't know if I'll stay until the end of my studies, perhaps even not until the end of this week, but for the moment, I'll agree to try again.

We started our daily routine again, and Marc kept his promise. He was kinder than ever and didn't make a single faux-pas. I, myself, still did what he expected of me, but not more. It was out of the question for him to imagine anything and to experiment with what I still thought of as extreme perversions. Our private games were limited to well-chosen put downs, some short and simple role-play with him at my feet and me threatening him with imaginary punishments. As promised, one day he suggested to me to come with him to his office, so that I could meet the people working with him and who also had a large network in the art business.

This could be very useful for my studies because I had to find a commercial internship for my second year at school, and so far my network in this field wasn't exactly extensive. Some of my classmates had family or acquaintances in the art business and that gave them a huge advantage in term of job opportunities. It was out of question for me to remain an outsider, when comparing myself to them and feeling the lack of equal opportunities. I actually had several days free to work on individual assessments and I decided to reserve one of these days to come to Marc's office. At the planned time, we took off early to his office which was situated a few streets away from the apartment in a district full of companies' headquarters and specialised in business related hotels. It was a real pleasure to share a slice of Marc's life like that. I felt valued and couldn't wait to discover the place where he was working. I found it very chic, very welcoming and at the same time, very simple, very similar to his apartment, though without the trinkets of course.

- Yes, I feel at home here. I wanted a place I could use for business but that also fits who I am.

His direct collaborators, an assistant, a decorator, and a sales representative had been working with him for several years and everybody seemed to appreciate their boss. Marc explained to me the mission he wanted to focus on and what he delegated to his team. His company had good results and he was thinking about establishing a subsidiary abroad in order to expand its development. After having called several people, he confirmed to me he could find an internship for me at one of his acquaintances companies - an art dealer. I was very happy with this news and I thanked him enthusiastically, amusing his colleagues with my country town naivety. I also met one of his clients coming for a job for a hotel in London, as well as his lawyer with whom he had an appointment. All that seemed fascinating to me and gave me the impression Marc was an experienced professional. Once again, I was admiring him. We had a quick lunch with the whole team in a nice café just around the corner from the office, and in the late afternoon, we both returned home after a busy but interesting day. In the car, I recollected with pleasure this whole fascinating day. How exciting his work was! However I had had been surprised by a conversation I overhead by accident, while Marc was talking with his lawyer, just before he left, with the door half open. I was sure I had heard him ask Marc how his wife was doing. I probably hadn't understood correctly, but it made me wonder if his colleagues knew what kind of private life he had and who he really was. None of them had asked questions about our relationship. They even didn't seem to be concerned about it, as if it was normal I was there for whatever reason. Even if I didn't want to take the risk to break our once more normal daily life, I allowed myself to ask a question.

- Marc, I would just like to know… you know, your colleagues, your acquaintances, all your relationships…
- What?
- Do they know about us? Do they also know you as privately as I do?
- Of course not, Laura. There are colleagues, as you said, and sexual partners. I don't mix different categories. I often take internships for students of your age, they're used to it.

The way he answered was firm enough to close the discussion.

Still quite disappointed and regretful about my experience in the nightclub, I was nicer and more tender with Greg on the phone, and decided to go back to Biarritz for the weekend, as my school had given us four days free.

With relief, I noticed my fiancé welcomed me with warmth. We were finding our intimacy once more, returning to old habits and were talking about our future.

- Another year in Paris und we'll be able to finally live together!
- It'll go fast. We could start looking for a little house.
- Let's wait to find a job first - it's more logical.
- You're right… though, I can't wait!

I felt good with him. I knew bad surprises would never happen with him, and it was reassuring. I had known Greg since Kindergarten and our parents, brothers and sisters were friends. We had grown up in good conditions, not rich but very well educated, like all the young people in our district. When we were kids, we were friends like many others, and it only was in high school that we had started getting closer, until we became inseparable. We shared common interests and enjoyed each other's company very much. Greg was a serious, healthy young man. He liked physical activities, not specifically for competition or muscles, but for well-being and the health it brings. He had hesitated between computer sciences and physical education but his need to move about and spend the majority of his time outside had been stronger. He couldn't see himself locked all day in an office with machines. Everything was simple with him because he had good common sense and didn't like confusing situations. Our temporary separation had made him feel very sad because I was living things he wasn't able to share with me and he had felt it was creating a gap between us. He told me he thought our love story was close to the end after my last visit. He hadn't dared to say anything, out of fear of worsening the situation, but he had spoken about it to his parents, explaining I had become very distant. He had needed to talk to them in order to be reassured. I realised just how much my behaviour had affected and even hurt him. I apologised, promising to be more careful from now on. Distance had confused me too. Now that we had talked about it, I was relieved and sure about my feelings. Everything made me feel guilty actually, because I hadn't told him the truth about my situation in Paris. Did I have to tell him everything about Marc? I couldn't continue to lie but it was impossible for me to admit to him the kind of relationship I was having with my landlord either.

"Actually, Greg, I have lied to you. My landlord is a sexual outsider who's into sadomasochism. He isn't old at all and the services I have to give him have nothing to do with the chores. He's renting for free and in exchange, I insult him and belittle him every day for his own pleasure."

No, really - I couldn't admit that to Greg after seven long months. Anyone would take me for an idiot, or worse, while listening to such a crazy story. And what would my parents say if they knew about it? For them, I was their dear daughter, so I couldn't imagine that - it would be the end of the world to them.

Coming back to my senses, the only solution I had, logically, was to break my agreement with Marc, find a suitable place to stay and live as cheaply as possible until the end of my studies. As soon as I returned to Paris, I would start looking for an apartment, and then I would inform my landlord of my departure. Then I wouldn't be keeping secrets from my loved ones and relatives anymore, and nothing would stop me from living the life I wanted. I would just have to say my landlord had wished to put an end to our agreement and it would be the last lie.

I felt completely convinced as I was taking the train to Paris, after having called Marc to confirm him the time of my arrival. When the train arrived at the station, he was patiently waiting for me on the platform, as the train was more than thirty five minutes late. I was confused he had to waste time waiting like that, but he reassured me it wasn't a problem, and that he preferred to pick me up rather than let me come home alone in the metro with my suitcase. His care was so touching, and I felt embarrassed by his attention. We made our way home without a word. It was the end of week-end and both of us were tired. Then, during dinner, he told me he would have to go away for a few days and he had to leave this evening.

- You have to leave for work?
- Not really, no. I go to visit a friend who's not doing too well.
- A friend?
- Yes, I have friends, you see. I'll be away for a few days, I'll call you to let you know when I will be back.

So I found myself alone in the apartment, which I didn't dislike because I had a lot to catch up on my personal researches I hadn't work on. I felt so good in this environment that I found neither the time nor the motivation to look for another apartment. I was studying hard, eating cold meals, only sleeping the bare minimum. I spent three days like that, very busy. The fourth day, as I was expecting to receive a call from Marc, I bumped into the neighbour from below us in the staircase. Despite her usual elegance, she was having trouble walking up the two steps separating the lift from the floor of her apartment. She looked depressed and unsure. I asked her if she needed help. She replied with a weak voice that she was recovering from the flu which had weakened her a lot. She thanked me, reassuring me everything was alright. I told her not to hesitate to knock on our door if she needed anything. She smiled and thanked me again. I wondered how such an attractive woman could be single. Later in the afternoon, Marc called me to say he would be back the next day, and I surprised myself by feeling so glad about it. To be honest, I was missing his presence in this vast apartment, even despite the services to provide, and I wasn't angry with him about that evening anymore. Now he looked to me like a much more complicated and complete human being, than just the aspect of his sexual preferences. That was a detail, after all, a minor part of his personality and of everything that I could he meant to me. Now it all seemed different, and I had the feeling not to judge things the same way here, in Paris, as when I was in Biarritz. Not long ago I wouldn't have thought such a thing, but actually, getting to know such a man was bringing me a lot.

His fine figure, his intelligence, his knowledge made me want to progress, to get better. I had never felt that before with anybody else. I loved Greg, who was a little like my alter ego, someone from my family, someone like me. But I admired Marc, who made me dream by opening doors to new perspectives of an exceptional life. And then, besides his clumsiness, he had always been so kind, so careful, so ready to satisfy my needs. More so than Greg perhaps.

I came back early the next day, in order to be there when he arrived. All day long I had tried to find something he would like for his return. I immediately had thought about preparing dinner because it was something I enjoyed doing and I had never had the opportunity to do it for him, as he always insisted on taking care of all the chores. First I was happy about my idea, but I quickly realised it was a mistake. Preparing anything that could be considered a chore wouldn't please him at all, because his pleasure was to be submissive, to submit and serve, not to be served. But what to do in then, if I wanted to make a present to someone like him? I wouldn't have to buy him a new torture toy, would I? I remembered different articles and explanations I had greedily read on the Internet on the day I had discovered the content of his drawers. By what I knew of him, a lot of situations that were mentioned in those articles might correspond to his taste.

Indeed, one of the described scenarios seemed like something I could manage. I would just have to use the dog leash, probably still in his bedroom. Hesitating, but pleased with my idea, I decided to take the thing and to try to see how it worked, to get used to it. First I was clumsy, then I used it with more confidence.

The idea of surprising him, of being the one initiating the action, the one having even more control over my partner, who desired just that, seemed to me an interesting experience - at least once. And well, if I wasn't going to try such a thing here, in Paris, the city of all possible perspectives, where would else I experience it?

CHAPTER VIII

Focused on my idea, I lost the sense of self-control I had imposed upon myself over the last few weeks, since our memorable evening in the nightclub. I could let myself go now, because soon I would be looking for another apartment. What I would do today would have only small consequences, so it would be a way to thank Marc and his professional help.

I went again over the whole scene I had prepared in my mind with the dog leash in my hand, letting the coat rack play the role of submissive partner. I had to fit the collar tightly around his neck, pull the leash firmly but with control, adjust the look in my eyes, play with my shiny red fingernails… The game, though it seemed daring, remained quite doable for me, and it didn't have any similarities with what I had seen in the nightclub.

It was around half past six when Marc arrived with a suitcase in his hand. I opened the door for him, and he smiled at me with a hint of fatigue. After having asked how his friend was doing, I went back to my desk and my exercise books, pretending to be concentrated. I was feeling extremely excited and my heart was beating very fast, but Marc wasn't aware enough to notice it. I saw him disappear for a moment into his bedroom where he changed clothes, then making his way to the kitchen to prepare dinner. After having judged, at a glance, that it was the right time, I impatiently left my seat and went to see him to ask for a glass of wine.

- I'm glad you're taking advantage of my wine stock, Laura. You're not doing it very often. I'll drink with you.
- Yeah, I've worked a lot while you were away, Marc, so I want to treat myself if that's okay with you.
- Of course, it's perfectly okay with me. It is even a sign of good health, and as for me, I need a treat too.
- Are you feeling sad for your friend?
- Yes, of course. But she'll surely get well soon. Now, how about we talk about something else, alright? What do you think about having a nice risotto?

Marc seemed worried. He had rings under his eyes, his face was pale, but he looked happy that I was taking some time to be with him. It was perfect for my surprise. We talked about decoration while he was preparing dinner, then about art during the meal. It was delicious. I was listening to him speak, I was drinking his words, he knew everything from the great masters of painting up to fashionable contemporary design brands. He looked very tired but it gave him a look of a man leading a mysterious life, with exciting nights, excess and pleasure. The wine made me tipsy and made me find him irresistible. I was waiting for him to finish clearing the table to start my plan, but he was taking his time and I couldn't wait anymore. I was like a little girl who couldn't wait until mother's day to show her drawing. Marc noticed I wasn't behaving as usual.

-   What's the matter Laura? Is everything alright?
-   Yes, very well Marc. I'm happy to see you, that's all.
-   Are you sure that's all? You look impatient, am I right?
-   Yes, you're right.
-   And … could you impatience miraculously be related to what I think?

-   That's entirely possible.

His tired face completely changed, his eyes lightened up and his entire person seemed to open right up. He seemed so happy. He looked at me in the eyes - that was the right time. I stood up, turned the lights down, went to fetch the leash and slowly came back to him without a word, letting it swinging from left to right in pace of my steps…

When I opened my eyes, it was black outside and the soft lights were still on in the apartment. I looked around. I was lying on the couch, in Marc's arms. I could feel his pulse against the side of my head. The clock said four o'clock.

I panicked and quickly dragged myself out of his arms when I realised the situation I was in, which I didn't judge appropriate. He didn't wake up anyway. He turned around and curled up against the leather in a foetus position with the leash around his neck, he was almost naked. Standing, I felt dazed and was looking everywhere around the room, looking for signs that would remind me what happened. I didn't have any clear memory of the evening. My brain wasn't working anymore, as if I had been swept away by a wave of madness. I only remembered the start of the scene, with me coming closer with the leash in my hand, and him, incredulous and greedy-eyed, looking at me with desire. I was still wearing the clothes I had chosen for dinner, with just one detail: my blouse was open. I quickly buttoned it up again, as if someone could suddenly arrive and see me like that, and then, not feeling like waking Marc, I hurriedly put a blanket on him and went to take refuge in my bedroom. I would have been unable to look at him like that, in this impossible, this crude and ridiculous situation. Feeling embarrassed, I preferred to escape and wait for him to get changed. So I took a shower in my bathroom, and parts of the evening started to come back. I succeeded in reconstructing more-or-less what could have happened, taking us to the point where I woke up, by remembering the scenario I had imagined when I was preparing my surprise and putting it together with the snippets of memory I could recollect. Marc tied up, under my control, his skin red from the knots, crying with pleasure, licking the metal, then going down to the ground… It looked unreal yet so present in my mind. In my flesh, I had wanted this situation to happen, I had sought it out, imagining this scenario - but I didn't think it would really happen. I had thought Marc would say stop, he wouldn't understand my change of behaviour, it wouldn't work because of my lack of experience…

But it had worked beyond my expectations, and I had fully participated in it. Worse, I still had a feeling of pleasure, or at least I had gotten pleasure from doing it for Marc. I probably had no regrets, and it was definitely time to rest after these emotions and to talk about it.

I almost immediately fell asleep, exhausted and disorientated, but happy.

Sunlight on my face brought me back to normal life, I had forgotten to close the shutters. I looked at my watch, it was half past eleven, and the smell of toasted bread wafted through the apartment, making me hungry.

After having put prude looking clothes on, I walked out of my bedroom. I went to the bathroom, then walked along the small corridor that led to the lounge and the kitchen. I could now recognise the smells of bacon and French toast, and I heard jazz like music in the background. When I got to the kitchen, the scene was astonishing. Marc, wearing his best bright linen clothes, bare feet, happy as never before, was cooking a delicious breakfast while dancing at the pace of his favourite music. The window in the kitchen was wide open, the sun was coming into the room, and everything gave the pleasant impression of holiday and happiness. I couldn't hold back a laugh, seeing this joyful scene. When he saw me, Marc laughed with me, and we both finished on a chair, hugging our belly, trying to calm down.

- Good morning Laura. Can I serve you? I have made a brunch, you might be hungry after this…
- Yes, I'm very hungry. Thanks Marc.

I interrupted him because I preferred him not to make any references to our evening for the moment while I had an empty belly and a mind still half asleep. We would enjoy this wonderful brunch and then we could discuss it.

We ate without a word exchanged, surrounded by the music and the sun, then I stood up and asked my partner to come to seat with me in the lounge. He followed me and sat in front of me in an armchair.

- Why are you so happy, Marc?
- I suppose this is the sun, the weekend, the joy of living.
- Is that all?

- No, it's probably not all. But do you want to talk about it?
- I think we should, yes. You know, I don't regret anything.
- Really?
- Yes, I had wanted what happened yesterday evening, and I enjoyed it.
- Are you sure? You're not saying that to please me?
- I wanted to please you, but I also had pleasure, the pleasure of giving you some.
- In that case, I'm happy.

We were now feeling the same. Marc held me in his arms, and kissed me, that was what I was waiting for.

This day was the beginning of a new kind of relationship between us. From now on, there was nothing else separating us - we had passed over the last barrier between us. We played our intimate games almost every evening, on my own initiative, or on his, imagined by him, or by me. I let myself create things and we both liked it. We were discovering unknown universes, new intense sensations. I went to my classes, which I followed with a little less concentration because I was thinking during the day of what we had done during the night. My classmates noticed my absent, sometimes asleep look. I invented I was giving evening courses to earn some money and I was going to bed very late. When Greg called, I behaved as nothing had happened. I didn't have any reason to be different - it was all just a game, a soon to be finished experience. The end of school year was near, and I knew well I had to go home for the holidays, and perhaps not returning to Marc's place after that. Having thought long enough about it, I decided not to look for another rent for the last few weeks left of the semester, despite what I had planned before. I didn't fear the moment of separation either, as my story with Marc was outside of reality. It seemed imaginary, it didn't interfere with my real life. At least, that was how I was looking at things.

For my studies, I had to prepare for an end of year assessment, a research project on contemporary art, about which I had to speak in my oral exam. I had chosen to speak about the legitimacy of certain contemporary artists like Jeff Koons or Paul McCarthy to be called artists and about their place in the actual global market. When Marc knew I'd be working on that, he helped me a lot. He took me to museums, introduced me to contemporary art specialists, bought me specialised magazines. I helped me in organising my research. It was a fantastic time, during which I had the impression of progressing, learning, coming to understand a lot better the sometimes superficial, sometimes deep art world, which so often was constituted almost only of chance and coincidence. Marc said artists who succeeded during their own lifetimes were the ones who found themselves at the right place at the right time, nothing more. The others were discovered after their death. I talked about talent which seemed important to me, but he responded that chance was the only real factor of being known. He liked baroque painters, especially Rembrandt and Rubens, though he said only contemporary photography could bring something new to art, because techniques had developed there which modified the work of the artists and was bringing them a freedom their predecessors didn't have.

Some days, depending on whether we both had free time, we would meet at lunch to talk about a certain subject in my research, then meet again at the end of the day for a visit to an art gallery, and finally, we would have dinner followed by an intense and intimate moment during which we fulfilled with each other's fantasies. We shared a lot and with great pleasure. It was an easy period of time where I completely let myself go. Nobody knew the kind of relationship we were having, nobody could imagine what was happening between us. This gave our relationship an incredible force, as if we were continuously fulfilling each other.

- Laura, you surprise me. Considering the way you reacted at the night show, I thought you would remain resistant to these kinds of things. I even thought you were going to leave me for ever.
- I wanted to, Marc. I didn't understand such an educated and pleasant man like could love such… crude games. But I know you better now. I'll stay until the holidays, if that's okay.
- Stay as long as you want, Laura. And I didn't know you found so many qualities in me…
- Well, actually, don't make any false expectations. I probably won't come back next year.

Marc seemed happy that I confided in him about my feelings, but disappointed I wouldn't be staying for my second school year. I had to say this agreement made me feel proud of myself, even flattered me.

- Perhaps you will change your mind in the end.
- I don't think so. You know I have a fiancé.

He didn't answer anything, the argument didn't resonate in his mind, or he preferred to forget about it. I suddenly remembered the discussion I had overheard with his lawyer some day before, I wanted to ask him if he had lived with someone, but I restrained myself. He didn't like talking about himself, and since I had told him I was going to leave, it was none of my business.

Weeks passed by the same way, almost euphoric, I was studying well, helped by my "guide", my teachers were happy about me and I trusted my future professional career. I came back to Biarritz a single time, persuaded by Greg who begged me to come home before the holidays. The weekend there was busy. There were a lot of acquaintances who were asking me how life is Paris was, if I was able to stand public transport, city life, stress, crowd, pollution. I was able to stand everything very well.

- But aren't you looking forward to come back home? You should feel alone in this enormous city with your old man.
- It's okay. You know, I study a lot, so I don't have time to get bored. And then, Parisians aren't that unpleasant, and the city is interesting.

- Don't you miss your family and Greg?
- Yes, of course.

How could I have been able to explain to them, without being arrogant, that I was leading an exceptional life, doing things I even couldn't have even imagined possible just a few months ago, when I was like them, persuaded real life was in quiet country towns. It was true that, when I was living there, with my family, without too many temptations, I had thought I had the best I could have, and felt safe. But, as I was used to it now, as soon as I set foot on the platform in Paris, my state of mind was changed, with a desire to discover and to experience, in all possible fields. That was the effect this city had on me.

CHAPTER IX

The last weeks quickly passed by quickly, and the daily routine was hectic. Each day, I was jumping from my studies to my - more and more frequent - intimate moments with Marc. Since I had let him know I wouldn't be coming back after the holidays, he seemed to want to take advantage of my presence even more so than usual, and was increasing the evenings out and intimate games. I didn't refuse a single one because I was sure I was gathering lots of experiences I wouldn't have again. My last few weak moral limits didn't resist, and I went beyond all reserve. I met a lot of different people, all interesting, in all kinds of situations, We went to all the places he knew and even some new ones with a certain pleasure, then, we came back exhausted but always very glad for having shared another moment together. Marc sometimes was carried me up from the car, where I had fallen asleep, to the apartment and I woke up in my bed the next morning, as if waking up from a comfortable dream.

I had my oral exam in mid-June, and Marc insisted to be there, which excited me a lot. I was embarrassed for not having suggested it in the first place, not having thought he would take it so seriously. My parents wouldn't be coming, as for them, travelling to Paris was a whole adventure and they had other things to do. I hadn't insisted because I would have had to introduce them to my "old" landlord. They were planning to come and visit me at the end of my second year and that suited me well. However, this oral exam was important because I had to present a research project I had been working on over the whole year, and I also wanted to make a good impression on Marc who had helped me to prepare this exam and who was my best support. My body was shaking a little bit when the jury gave me the signal to start, but Marc was looking at me with so much trust and pride that I quickly found the strength I needed. Feeling encouraged by his support, I obtained the best mark, far beyond the others. After the exam, I jumped into his arms to kiss him on the cheek and to thank him. He looked moved.

- Laura, that was wonderful! Let us celebrate with dignity - let me invite you for dinner at the restaurant.
- Marc, the last time you invited me to the restaurant…
- Come on, I really want to make it nice this time. Restaurant and theatre, just nice and normal things.

We laughed, while climbing up the stairs leading to the apartment after my exam to get changed before going out. I had called Greg just before, then my parents to tell them everything had gone well and I had passed my exam. They were very happy for me and were looking forward to seeing me for the holidays. I still had a few days of classes, and then I would have to leave. Marc kindly told me he preferred not to think about it, that we should live the present moment.

Our evening was perfect, there weren't any bad surprises this time, but it was a feast for the taste buds, for the eyes and for the mind. When we came home, just after one o'clock in the morning, Marc took my hand with softness and sensuality and brought me to his bedroom. We spent the whole night embraced in his bed.

For the last days, my personal "guide" was often away. He didn't give any explanation, but let me understand he preferred to slowly separate himself from me rather than find himself abruptly without me. I found that so charming, so touching. Could it be that he was feeling something for me and that my departure really made him sad? The closer the time of our separation came, the less time we were spending together – at the very least, just dinner. With my classmates, some of whom wouldn't come back the next year because they had failed in their exams, we had organised a big party to say goodbye. As we were having a drink together to finish the party, I explained I would have to find another rent. One of the girls told me she also had to find somewhere else because her landlord was sick and wouldn't be taking anybody anymore in the apartment. I was thinking for myself Marc would perhaps be interested if I sent him a new student, but this idea was of course unrealisable and I quickly got rid of it. I actually couldn't have borne knowing this young woman I was friends with was taking my role. That wasn't possible, the relationship I had with Marc was unique - who else could satisfy him like me? She, herself, suggested another solution.

- We could look for a rent together, if you want, Laura. It could be easier to find an affordable flat.
- You're right. If you like, we can speak about it at the end of July, at the right time to begin looking for one. We'll get in touch. That's a good idea.

It was Tuesday, and I had to go to Biarritz the next day. It was half past six, I was almost finished packing my things, and I was waiting for Marc for our last dinner together. Being mysterious as usual, he told me that for this last evening, he had planned to prepare something special, a new recipe, which he hoped would leave me an with unforgettable memory, so that "I would go with regrets". These few words made me laugh, but Marc wasn't really joking, there was sadness in the tone of his voice. He really had hoped I would tell him I had changed my mind, and would see him again for the next school year, but I couldn't. If I was playing his game, indulging his fantasies, it was for curiosity, not for taste. If I liked what we were doing together, it was because he liked it, and I liked seeing him happy. Now, it was time to go back to normal life. To show him he was important for me, I actually wanted to buy him a present and I immediately thought of a very beautiful lamp he had noticed in a shop around here, while we were walking together. It cost a fortune. I had never bought a decoration object that expensive. But when I went to the shop again to see the lamp, it seemed to me that was the least I could do for a man who had welcomed me like a queen and opened his door, and finally, his arms. So I bought the lamp, which I asked to be carefully wrapped and which I took home with pride and care.

Marc finally arrived a little before eight o'clock. I had had time to make myself beautiful, and for this last evening, I was wearing the close-fitting black dress he liked and which I had taken back after having thrown it in the rubbish bin after the evening in the nightclub. There again, I had used a little of my money to have the dress laundered, so that it would be carefully cleaned and ironed. He seemed to appreciate the effort, complimented me and told me that, for our last dinner, we wouldn't have to do anything, neither him nor me. We would just have to sit at the table and be served by a famous chef, as well as friend and customer, who he had hired for the occasion. He only asked me a few minutes to make himself good-looking too.

- I want to fully enjoy your presence, Laura. So, tonight, we'll have dinner just the both of us.

- That's wonderful! I didn't even know it's possible to do something like that! Wow, being served by a famous chef at home!

I was very pleased by the idea because having dinner without playing submissive games made me very happy. I often had wanted it without ever suggesting it, and at last, it was him offering it to me, and in an exceptional situation at that.

- I have a present for you, Marc.
- Really?

I picked up the lamp, which was wrapped in a silver paper with a black laced up ribbon all around it. Marc tore off the paper like a kid, and seemed enchanted when he saw his present.

- Laura, you shouldn't have bought that. It's gorgeous! I love it! Thanks. I accept it with no embarrassment because I know you will soon be rich, because you're very talented, believe me.

He kissed me, then served me a glass of champagne, while the chef, who had just arrived, was getting busy in the kitchen. He turn the lights down, put a kind of music I liked, and came to sit next to me.

- Thanks for everything, Laura.
- But it's me who should thank you. You've done so much for me.
- No, you're wrong. You've offered me your presence, your understanding, your generosity. It's so much more than I was expecting.

Dinner, which lasted several hours, was a wonder. He was right, I would never forget this evening. Around half past eleven, the chef left us after having shared the dessert with us and some cooking secrets. We just had to enjoy the rest of the night now.

- Are we going to sleep together?
- I would prefer to stay here, on the sofa, Laura. It would be too difficult to let you go tomorrow otherwise. If it's okay, I'm not going to take you to the station. I don't really like saying goodbye. I'll call a taxi for you.

So we lay down on the black leather sofa which represented an important symbol now, of our secret agreement but also of our most intimate moments. We comfortably fell asleep against one another under a light cotton blanket.

So the next day, I left alone, in the taxi Marc had called. He had left before I woke up, leaving only a little note with the time my driver would pick me up, and after his name, he had written, again with mystery, "useless memory of an unforgettable parenthesis". Had he slept with me all night on the sofa? I would never know. I also left him a note on his desk.

"Take care of yourself. I'll think of you, my dear Marc."

It was the first time I was being so sentimental.

I arrived early at the station, my train was taking off at quarter past twelve, and it was eleven twenty five. I bought an art magazine and a bottle of water, but didn't take anything to eat. I had an unpleasant lump in my throat and felt unable to eat any food. The memory of Marc's skin against mine was still very present in me, the sensations, the softness as well as the violence were mixed all together in the fever I was feeling growing inside of me like a wave. I remained a few hours in this state, still but boiling on my seat, until a neighbour in the train asked me if I had finished my magazine and if he could read it. I answered him that actually I still hadn't started it, and asked him if he was working in the art field. He was florist in Paris but came from a little city, close to mine, and was very interested in painting. We discussed some points of view, and then I got up to freshen myself up. In the tiny toilet, I looked at myself in the mirror. My hair was still too long, and it seemed to me I had lost weight since I had left Biarritz the year before. My white blouse was a bit too baggy on my chest. Someone knocked on the door, a lady wanting to use the toilets. I went back to my seat and opened my magazine. Along the pages, numerous articles were referring to artists or art trends I now knew well, for having listened so much to Marc talking about it. I even noticed a mistake where it talked about an artistic style. This concentrated reading slowly calmed me down, and without noticing, I fell asleep. My florist neighbour woke me up as we were arriving to the station and he was getting ready to get out too. I followed the crowd leading to the exit. When I saw once more my usual environment, the buildings, the shops, with my heavy suitcases in my hands, I immediately felt pulled back a year ago. I wasn't Marc's partner anymore, I was the country girl again, Greg's fiancé. Or better said, I was both, in different places and different times. What surprised me was that I was living this duality so easily, without feeling the need to justify myself or to feel guilty about what happened during this school year. It happened, that's all, it happened because I had wanted it, and if I had to choose whether or not to do it again, I would do it. And now, the only thing that made me feel unsure was whether I explain my story with Marc to Greg or not. Spontaneously, I wanted to tell him, not to make him suffer or to give myself value, nor even for him to despise me and leave me, but because for me, it just been a flirt, a discovery opportunity, a way to grow up faster, to have new and interesting experiences. I would have told him as if I was talking about a journey I had made with someone else and wanted to share what happened during the trip.

"You know, it was fantastic. I was like, pushed into this strange relationship. It was like, living with Marc every day had forced me to open myself, to receive and collect everything life in Paris had to offer."

But it was impossible to talk about it with Greg. No, I had to keep secret this *unforgettable parenthesis,* as Marc had appropriately called it – a phrase aside from the main flow of my life, to be put in brackets.

Speaking about Greg, he was walking straight toward me from the station square, a big smile on his face. He walked with a straight tread, looking directly at me – almost naively according to what a Parisian would have said – and opened his arms and hugged me firmly without wanting to stop. I felt good in his arms. I was finding again the man I had left behind a few months ago, as if nothing had happened. Without saying anything, he picked up my suitcases and we made our way to the parking lot.

CHAPTER X

Summer started well. Country town life, pace, solitude, state of mind - everything was slower and more structured down here. My parents had transformed the little hut in the garden that used to be used by my father to keep his tools. At that time, he was doing more work at home, even after a whole day at the factory. He didn't use it anymore because of tiredness and lack of interest. He now preferred his armchair and his newspaper, so he had sold his tools. The hut had been rebuilt, repainted in white on the outside and white and blue on the inside, soberly furnished with a big comfortable sofa bed and a little bedside table, equipped with electricity for light and a beautiful shelf, full of books. It was a real nest, a welcoming cocoon where you can rest and read. And make love.

- It's for Greg and you. Now that you're getting married, you need at least a little home before finding a house. You can isolate yourselves when you need to.
- It's great, thanks Dad.

I actually noticed that during my time away, everybody had made lots of projects for the future of our couple, and I suspected Greg hadn't slowed them down. So in his family as well as mine, everybody was only speaking about us, our life as a couple, our wedding, each of them was making their suggestion or offer, and my brothers and sisters were busy getting information from their local friends. There was always someone who knew a good band, or a great florist, or the best delicatessen shop, and they were thinking of helping writing the wedding announcements, organising the table seats.

I was finding it all a little bit hasty, and couldn't refrain myself letting Greg know.

- Don't you think we should first get a job?
- Yes, of course, but it's only a question of time. I should be able to quickly find a job as sports trainer around here, outside of my class hours. The guy employing me this summer has already

confirmed it. And then, everybody would be so happy to help organise our wedding. You know well that it's better to start preparing it a year before, or even earlier, to organise such a big event. You'll have plenty of time to finish your studies by next year. What do you think?
- Yes, that's entirely possible. Well, putting it like that, it's sounds good.
- Are you sure? You don't look that enthusiastic!
- Of course, Greg, I'm very glad to be getting married with you!

We still had a few days free before starting our summer jobs, he as a personal trainer at a holiday club and me in a rental agency, where I had worked each summer since I was seventeen. Thanks to these summer jobs, we were able to cover some of our school fees, helping our parents. I was particularly motivated this time because I knew that the coming year would be financially difficult for me. Even in a flat, I would need at least four hundred fifty euros per month for a rent and food, transport… and that was only the necessities, without any additional spending money, not for going out, or even for a cup of coffee. My limited savings would suffer, and my parents would still need to help me out, perhaps with up to hundreds of euros. I didn't even offer myself a visit to the hairdresser, conscious about my savings this summer, instead just asking my mum to trim the ends. I wanted to keep my hair long, even if it was less practical. Marc had often told me how much he liked it long.

- It's such a pity your landlord is moving. It'd be almost impossible to find such good opportunity again, so much comfort in Paris!
- For sure, I struck gold. Let's just say I was lucky to have had such an advantage for the year… But I'll find something else. And now I know the city a little better, and have a few tips.

My family and friends often asked me questions about the capital city - how people live, how do people manage to not get lost on the metro, are the monuments really that beautiful…? I happily answered their questions, and insisted on the fact that most people in Paris spent a lot of time at work and in transport and that the majority of them were used to go to the same places - their home, their workplace, and one or two places where they liked to relax according to their taste, like a park, a cinema or a restaurant. All very routine, really. My parents were probably fascinated, while perhaps also a little afraid, imagining an always full and stressful life. I tried not to argue about it as, after all, my point of view was actually different, because of Marc.

I often thought about him, especially when I was reading one of these countless art or decoration books I had borrowed from the library. I read these avidly on the beach or in our little shack in the garden, while Greg was leafing through magazines about sport, cinema or computers. Carried by the general enthusiasm, we were planning moving-in projects together, dreaming of a modern house close to the sea, which we could furnish as we liked, cooking nice meals, inviting our parents, brothers and sisters, and friends for lunch. Yet, at the same time, I found myself asking what Marc was doing, all alone in his apartment, and had all sorts of questions running through my mind. Had he already have found someone to replace me? Was he going out each night? Was he cooking delicious dinners for him alone? Would I be able to see him again? Better not to think too much about it.

The days passed by slowly, filled with visits to the beach, with our friends, our family meals, our stays in the shack, and our discussions about future. I was feeling very well, supported, loved, confident. What more could I ask for, than the job of my dream, and my days spent with the man of my life? I was in my environment, in my place.

After this break, we had to jump into our summer job. It actually felt like a proper job, with of the amount of hours and the intensity. I appreciated seeing my former colleagues again, and I was doing everything I could to get the best bonus on summer house rentals. I had decided it would be like a game, a single extra euro earned meant another point for comfort for the next year – points towards a better meal, or a time out with my classmates... I was going back to Greg in the evening in our little cabin, after dinner with his parents or mine, and together we slept there exhausted but happy, almost every night. Yet, there was just little problem which concerned our love relationship, and in particular, moments when we were making love. Greg was a very soft, kind and gentle guy, and that was a thing I had always considered as natural, and I appreciated it. I even know some of my friends, when we happened to talk about our sexual experiences, had been with men a little brutal or only concentrated on their own pleasure, and they envied me a lot for being with someone so tender. I agreed, but from time to time I would have liked Greg to be a little more direct with me, not always asking me my opinion - I wanted him to take without asking. I didn't dare to speak to him about it, though.

No news from Marc. He was respecting our tacit agreement, not contacting me again since I had decided not to come back to him.

One weekend, at the end of July, with two weeks to work for Greg and me, I finally started looking for a rent for the new semester. My parents had reminded me a few times already that it was time to look for a new room, but I had postponed it as late as I could, as I wasn't very eager to motivate myself for rent hunting. I finally decided to contact my classmate who had suggested to me that the two of us share a flat together. I had both her cell phone number and the number for her parents' home, where she was supposed to be staying for a month or so. As I couldn't reach her on her mobile, I tried calling the second number, but her parents told me she had had a health issue at the beginning of the holidays and they weren't sure if she would be going back to Paris for the coming year, as the treatment demanded a lot of rest. I was unsure; I didn't really have the choice to wait for her to get better. After having made sure she wasn't badly sick, I told her parents to wish her a speedy recovery and she shouldn't hesitate to call me as soon as possible. This was bad news for my plans, because I really was relying on her help, but I had to find a new idea.

I was found myself once more hostage to the hunt for housing, this difficult and uncertain quest. Where would I have to start this time? What would I have to do in order to make the most of my time and obtain a decent result, all without being there in Paris? The answer came quite fast, as having already experimented with this search I knew normal methods wouldn't pay off, except by crazy chance. I would have to look into service exchanges, non-standard offers, sometimes weird looking offers... certainly dubious, but only for someone who had never tread this ground before.

I made a list of key words corresponding to the offers which, I thought, could help me better sort out what I was looking for, rather than the same old standard offers promising a *furnished studio, close to the RER city train, in good state and at low cost*. My list included, among others, words like: services, exchange, free rent, offer, SM. It's not that I wanted to get in that sort of stuff again, purposely looking for the same conditions, but it just was easier like that, because I was initiated, and I had to at least use this skill.

For several hours I sat staring at my screen as I looked for a rent, going over results from my requests, sorting through, selecting, trying to analyse what could be hidden behind the words, remembering those which Marc or his acquaintances used to use. There was a whole vocabulary that only belonged to this sphere, with a lot of nuances corresponding to very precise actions and letters, even numbers sometimes. There weren't that many offers, but if I had to choose one or two, I wanted them to be the most affordable for me, in fact, the most moderate ones.

One of them seemed particularly interesting, with a pretty vague but nice title: "Offer comfortable rent for reasonable service".

So I decided to call and a feminine voice answered, not belonging to the person who had posted the offer, as she told me. She explained to me the conditions of the offer, which was proposing free rent in a decent place, in return for giving the landlord some of my time, about three hours per week, during which he demanded friendly company mainly for reading. I shyly tried to ask on phone if this reading had to do with a specific topic, but the woman answered she would tell me more during a visit we had to organise.

So I quickly had to plan a travel to Paris if I didn't want someone else grabbing it before me. There again, I hated having to lose a big part of my recent savings for this trip. Greg, having heard me complaining, offered to pay half of the ticket, but I refused because he needs his savings as much as I did. After a slightly agitated night, being anxious I would not arrive early enough, I thought about the offer in the train. What secret could hide the mysterious landlord who didn't even answer personally on the phone? Was he deaf, or didn't he dare to present his offer himself? What kind of reading could he be expecting, for him to offer such a place for no cost? Rent payments, even in a flat, really represented a considerable income. When I arrived at the place, I noticed the street the woman had indicated to me didn't quite have the same charm as Marc's quarter – situated a few kilometres away – but it sure would be pleasant living there. A lot of shops, a library and a swimming pool were all in the locale, of the somewhat old but decent looking building. With a reserved enthusiasm, I went up the stairs to the indicated floor, knocked on the door and found a middle-aged lady holding out her hand to me.

- Hello miss, are you coming for the rent offer? I'm the landlord's sister, I talked to you on the phone. I live a few streets away from here. Come in. My brother won't take too long, he's just getting changed. He wants to look his best to meet you.
- Thank you.

We entered in what would have been the lounge, a little dark and soberly furnished, but welcoming nonetheless. The lady was well dressed, reserved, though wearing some beautiful jewellery adding some glamour. She seemed to have paid attention to her appearance.

- I've helped my brother to clean all morning. I didn't want you to be scared. He's a little bit boorish because he almost doesn't go out anymore, but he loves reading. The problem is that he doesn't see very well anymore and reading tires him a lot, so I come by from time to time to read a book with him, but I can't satisfy his appetite for reading. In short, we've received a good education if quite strict. Our parents didn't allow us a lot of time to dream or to read. My brother had kept a strong feeling of frustration from that time, and as soon as he could, he has spent basically all of his whole free time in libraries. Now that he's retired, he feels awful if he doesn't read at least one or two books per week. When he suddenly had his eyesight damaged due to an eye disease, we thought of a way to still provide him the only pleasure which keeps him alive. And I thought of this solution: to welcome a student who would read for him, in exchange for a place to stay rent-free. He's been living alone for a long time, but he is still very motivated by the idea, because as he says, he can't live without books. The apartment is big - two people can easily live there without disturbing each other. And if it makes things easier for a young lady while she's studying, that's perfect!

- It's… it's a really good idea. Are there any genres he really likes?
- No, not at all. Everything interests him. He's insatiable, he will never get bored to discover new books. Do you like reading ?
- Yes, a lot. I don't have a lot of time because of my studies but I definitely like reading.
- So, it's perfect. Oh, here we are, here comes my brother.

The man was impressive. He was tall and big. About sixty years old, with grey hair and clear eyes, wearing thick glasses. He walked like a much younger man, though with a little hesitation in his behaviour, probably because of this visual defect. He was wearing ochre velvet pants and a subtle blue shirt, perfectly ironed and hemmed with red. He came closer, hesitating to shake my hand.

- Hello Miss. My name is Rodolphe Pardon.
- Hello Sir, I'm Laura. Nice to meet you.
- Are you a student?
- I study art, very close from here.
- I know the school – it's a very good school. I was administrative officer in the ministry of education, looking after applications for finance for school cafeterias. Anyway, I'm looking for a motivated and passionate person who likes to read. My eyes aren't as good as before.

The man looked shy and I understood why his sister was looking after the calls from candidates.

- We've only received two more calls since we've put the offer online, yesterday morning, but the other person will only come late evening. You're the first.

After having made me sit on an armchair in front of them, Rodolphe Pardon and his sister, almost one after the other, explained to me in detail how they were imagining the readings would take place, how often and for how long. Half an hour sessions, up to three quarter of an hour, five to six times a week, preferably in the evening, though it could be arranged according to my availability. The session would be timed and written down in a notebook in order to guarantee the equality of the exchange. Being aware a student needed time for personal study, they had limited their demands to three hours per week added up, even if Rodolphe would have appreciated having longer sessions. His sister reminded him it was already good having thought of this solution, as it was allowing them to avoid paying someone.

- And for meals? I have lunch at school but for dinners?
- We suggest to you to have it together, if that's okay with you. My sister comes every day to deliver my meals. She'll prepare something for you, too. We'll ask you for a little contribution of two euros, if that's alright.
- That would be perfect.

After that, Rodolphe Pardon's sister suggested me to look around the apartment, which looked bigger than it seemed, she was right.

- Yes, my brother likes large rooms. Here, he has three rooms for himself alone. The rent is a little expensive for his pension, but that's the price of comfort. In any case, that's how he likes living his life. Because he spends almost his entire days here, it's important he has enough room. I don't really want him to go out alone, he could trip over something and hurt himself.

I could imagine myself in this place without a problem. The bedroom which I would be renting was big, bright and well oriented, and the furniture was of the same style as the rest of the apartment - a little old fashioned, but perfectly fitting the man's personality. There already was a desk set up in a corner, perfect for studying. I would just have to add a nice little lamp and a colourful bedspread to make everything look charming. The question I had in mind was to whether it would work living together, considering the man had always lived alone. But hesitation was a luxury I couldn't afford, and if I was going to be chosen, I would quickly have to show my interest.

- I'm in. If you agree, we can sign the contract.

CHAPTER XI

As soon as I got out of Rodolphe Pardon's house, I took a deep breath, taking a moment to observe the street, the people walking around, the neighbourhood. The man had just confirmed his choice to accept me, asking his sister to cancel the second visit, which was planned for the evening, and to remove the offer from online. Our contract would be prepared with my name, address and phone number in the next few days, and would be sent to my address in Biarritz. I would just have to sign it and send it back. I didn't have to worry about anything, we had had an agreement.

"I've done well", I thought. "I'll feel at home here."

With all these comings and goings, the atmosphere of the street brought me back in my recent memories of Paris, still fresh in my mind. I was covering them with a veil of decency, though, as if I was trying to put some distance between me and them. Yet, unwillingly, I was seeing myself back at Marc's place, working at the wooden desk while he prepared dinner, as the linen veils in the lounge were undulating in the light and the proximity between each other sometimes stirring our imagination to go beyond boundaries. Of course, the comparison with Monsieur Pardon's house was not at the same level, as the service I was expected to do didn't exactly demand the same level of involvement - at least not from what I had understood with his sister's explanation. Having been at first surprised, I had slowly become amused during the visit. Throughout the first part of the interview, as we sat in the lounge, as she was explaining me the origin of the idea, I was almost expecting a confession about some kind of other motivation, a more or less shameful habit, perhaps a strong taste for young women or something else. All my thoughts were actually quite far from reality, and I even felt embarrassed for having so surely imagined that there might have been something of that sort in this man's offer. It was funny to feel so wrong. Apparently then, not all offers posted on non-official websites were based on some sort of deviant sexual desires! Spending three hours a week reading to a book loving man, in exchange for a decent and well situated place to stay seemed completely fine to me. I really was so lucky and my parents as well as Greg, to whom I wouldn't have to lie this time, would be astonished and relieved. As was I.

Before going to the station, I allowed myself a coffee break, to sit down and appreciate this feeling of satisfaction, and to congratulate myself for this visit. I had been at the time well inspired and well organised, which had given me a good result beyond my initial hopes. Marc would have been proud of me.

What… why was I thinking of Marc at this moment? Why would he be more proud of me than my own parents or my fiancé? Was it the influence of being back in the city bringing me unconsciously back to the one who had supported me during my exam, showing me how much he believed in my abilities? Indeed I had often thought that I owed him a big part of my success at that exam, and I was very grateful towards him.

Back at my parent's place, I confirmed to them with pleasure the good news I already had mentioned over the phone. I had found a new place to rent and it wouldn't cost me anything else than a few hours reading at a shy old man's side. I surprised everyone in the family, and my brother even started calculating all the money I would save over my two years of study thanks to my *free rent offers,* as he called them!

-   You really are resourceful - it's incredible how lucky you are! Paris sure is a difficult city to live in for old people, who might feel very lonely to accept your company!

August passed quietly by. Study, beach, family and friends, everything seemed perfectly balanced, as if it were all synchronised towards a single goal: preparing me for a second successful educational year. I rarely had had the opportunity since childhood to feel this sensation of everything going according to my plans, everything falling into place to make my life easier.

This feeling only lasted for a short period because at the time, and almost without me or my willing involvement, the wedding was getting organised. My mother was suggesting to me to collect magazines for wedding dresses in order to help me get an idea and make a first choice. The budget was tight, all the money should be carefully spent. I had to sit, whether I liked it or not, browsing these magazines displaying smiling young women with teeth as white as their dresses. Instead of being able to identify with them, I didn't feel like they corresponded to the idea I had of myself. Actually, that was the only question that, at that time, which paradoxically became more and more difficult to answer, as everything was being planned for me – who was I? Well, I was a young fulfilled student, alright; a country town girl, okay; I had a fiancé with whom I was getting married the next year, and I had professional career ambitions. But I knew that underneath the idyllic appearances, I would have to combine those great things with a personal life that seemed to take a now somewhat uncontrolled direction.

Anyway, I was trying to force myself to imagine myself in one of those wonderful, immaculate dresses, walking with my hand on Greg's arm in front of the whole jubilant family. Yes, that was a nice image. That was nice - but it wasn't me. Or more precisely, yes, that was me, here in Biarritz, but not me in Paris.

Greg appeared at this moment in the lounge, after his sport.

- Oh, I see you're starting to think about your dress! Don't tell me anything, I want to see it for the first time on our wedding day! I'll let you decide for yourself.

Around the end of August, it was now time to prepare everything to head back to the capital. I packed my things with excitement, all my attention being concentrated on the activity, which signified to me a return to hard but enthusiastic intellectual studies. Which clothes would be the most appropriate? I now had two kinds of clothes. There were those I usually wore here, in the countryside, in which my family and friends were used to seeing me - simple and practical. And there were those I had bought a year ago, when I was getting ready to go to Marc's place, and which were of a much better quality. I hadn't worn them since my return to Biarritz, and nobody here had ever seen me wearing them, as I didn't care to explain why Parisians deserved a classier look from me than my own family. I actually couldn't explain this fact to myself, except with a basic need for integration or something like that. I decided to take them with me - I would wear them again when I would get my first job. My parents offered me a very nice pen to keep me company during my studies, as they said. I thanked them warmly, happy to hold in my hands this present, full of affection, that I would use at every opportunity. On the departure day, Greg brought me to the station and passionately kissed me. By his own words, he was thinking of visiting me as soon as I was free, because he was missing me already.

In the train, I called Rodolphe Pardon to confirm my arrival time. He warmly answered, as if he was waiting for me impatiently. He had received the signed contract, everything was alright, and my room was ready. For courtesy, I brought a present for him in my suitcase, a speciality from my region, a box of Mouchous®.

After the journey, which seemed long and boring, I finally reached my destination and rang the doorbell at my new landlord's place. His sister was there with him and both were waiting in the lounge, probably discussing my arrival and the last organisation details. They greeted me with a big smile and thanked me for the present, and then offered me a little something to eat which had been prepared by Jeanne. I had already eaten in the train, but out of politeness, I didn't refuse the piece of quiche or the drink, both offered with insistence. It was late though, so I thanked them for the meal and told them I needed to rest. I still wanted to put my things in order and prepare myself before going to sleep. I started my courses the next day at ten o'clock and I still had things to organise. The sister spontaneously hugged me, letting me know I could call her Jeanne, and Rodolphe Pardon shook my hand, wishing me good night's sleep. He told me reading would only start after a week, so that I would have time to organise myself, according to what had been written in our agreement. He seemed very strict, according to the document I had received at my parents' place during the holidays, which included close to ten full pages. Inside, everything was detailed, from the room where readings would take place to the list of expenses my landlord would take care of: water, electricity, small few expenses… all this had impressed my family a lot. A remnant of his job, perhaps.

The week was intense. After a joyful return with the majority of first year students, among whom I didn't see my sick classmate who was recovering at her parent's place, a demanding and difficult program for the year was presented to us. It included a whole lot of assignments to be completed at very close dates. This suited me well because these assignments demanded finding companies, and I would be pleased to build upon the number of contacts I had made by and large thanks to Marc's network. I also planned to return back home four times in the year, as I had let my new landlord know with the potential dates of my travels written down in our contract. At first, I was a little bit confused by this very precisely planned and rigid lifestyle, which was carefully organised, recorded and detailed. Now I was allowing this structure to help me concentrate more fully on my studies. And after all, my new landlord didn't know me and from what I could understand from his personality, it was logical he was being so careful.

In daily life, Rodolphe Pardon was a discrete man, as I had imagined him to be. He didn't get up very early and it was rare that I saw him in the morning before going to my classes. When I came back in the evening, around half past six, he normally was taking the washing in, filling in cross words, specially adapted to his weak eyes, or busy in some other activity at home. He didn't seem to get bored, always said hello with the same enthusiasm. Then after around an hour, which I would spend getting changed and relaxing, he would call me for dinner. Meal time was a quiet time, during which we hardly spoke neither of us would dare to start a long conversation, whatever the topic. We ate meals prepared and brought the same day by Jeanne, while I was in class. There were traditional family meals, cooked with care, and things like tarts and fresh fruit salads. I loved them.

- Jeanne is a very good cook.
- Yes, she had always liked cooking. Well, I would be very capable of doing it too because our parents taught both of us the same things, but she insists and I know she likes doing it for me, so I let her do it. And of course, I can't see very clearly anymore, so this is an advantage too.
- Have you always been living here since you left your parents?
- At first, we were living together, Jeanne and me, in a three room apartment nearby, but when she met her husband, of course, we separated. Since then, I've been living here alone. It has been forty five years now. Are you feeling at home?
- Very well, yes, thank you. It's perfect. We'll start reading on Sunday, won't we?
- That's right, at five, for three quarters of an hour. I suggest a novel from Georges Simenon to start, The Widow Couderc. I haven't read it for a long time.

Rodolphe Pardon didn't seem to want to know more about me. It didn't disturb me, even though I imagined it was very difficult for him, according to his personality, to welcome into his apartment someone he didn't know at all. No doubt, the idea of having someone to read for him had proved stronger in his mind, than continuing his normally solitary habits. Jeanne had asked me some questions about my family situation during my first visit, though without showing a lot of curiosity either. Yet, it was the first time they were taking a student, and other landlords would surely have been more cautious. When I had moved in at Marc's place, it's true that he didn't ask a lot about me, but the context was different. Completely different.

On Saturday, I got up late, enjoying my first morning of rest since my arrival. I was tired because of the classes, travels and my busy new schedule, and relaxing in bed was good for me. I took my breakfast listening to the news. Rodolphe Pardon had been up for a while and Jeanne was meant to be coming to bring the meals of the day. On weekends, it was planned that I would eat at the apartment for both lunch and dinner.

- My sister will probably stay with us for lunch. She often does. You'll see - she'll come in, saying she's in a hurry, she's just passing by, and then, she'll sit to drink a glass of water and finally, I'll offer that she eat with us. She'll refuse at first, then she won't resist the temptation. Her husband is used to it, he won't wait for her and often eats alone on the weekend for lunch, he knows she's with me.

Things went exactly as he had said, almost according to the letter. This amused me, and I was glad Jeanne had invited herself into our daily routine. I liked watching both of them. I could feel the strong complicity between them which unites a brother and a sister who have together faced adversity and shared joy, who also have lived together at ages when usually siblings separate, and who did for each other like for themselves. I told them.

-   We're twins. You can't see it, can you? We're really twins!

Indeed, I couldn't see it at all because they were so different physically. Jeanne was smaller and skinnier, and her face was round with almost green eyes. Rodolphe Pardon was tall and big, bony, and his eyes were bright blue. I was very surprised. Jeanne smiled and served me a cup of coffee.

-   I hope you feel comfortable here. It's important to feel good to study well. Don't hesitate to tell us if you need something. My brother won't automatically think of everything, but he'll do anything you want if you ask him. He's a very nice man, you know.

I spent two pleasant days preparing for my courses of the coming week, walking a little bit through the quarter, having lunch with my hosts, and simply taking advantage of the comfort of the house. I called my parents and Greg, who seemed not to be worrying about me. They knew I was able to deal with my life alone because I already had done it before, with success. On Sunday, around four o'clock, just as I was coming home after a long walk, close to the apartment's door, I thought I saw Marc driving along the street. He wasn't living so far away from here, so it was possible he was the one driving but he didn't seem to recognize me when he turned his head towards me, and I concluded I was wrong. Sometimes I wanted to call him, to suggest that see each other, to go have a drink, but I didn't dare. He hadn't done it and perhaps it was better like that.

Five o'clock was approaching this Sunday, and feeling a little anxious I was preparing for the reading. According to the agreement, Rodolphe Pardon would bring the book to the lounge, and we would sit in front of each other, on the sofa close to the window for me while he sat back on a green armchair. He had removed every visible object on the surrounding furniture, in order not to disturb the reading, and had unplugged the phone. The curtain was covering the window a little, letting light penetrate inside, just a little but enough to read clearly.

Now I could start.

CHAPTER XII

"He was walking. He was alone, over three kilometres at least, on a road that was diagonally cut every ten meters by the shadow cast of a tree's trunk. Making big steps, yet without hurry, he made his way from one shadow to the next. As it was almost midday and the sun was coming close to the zenith, a short, ridiculously stocky shadow, his own, drifted along before him.[1]"

I had never read The Widow, even though I had already heard about it and the title was familiar to me. Georges Simenon wasn't one of my favourite authors, but I appreciated his writing from the first sentences of the novel, as if the circumstances could influence my perception of the book. The solemnity that surrounded our *tête-à-tête* and the setting imagined by my landlord were bringing us closer to meditation, and made this moment and the story precious.

Rodolphe Pardon, my single audience member, was all ears. He was sitting straight in his armchair, dressed with well ironed beige pants and blue shirt.

[1] Translator's own translation of the text from the novel The Window Couderc from Georges Simenon

He had put his glasses away and his face looked completely different to me, revealed like that. I could see a little bit of Jeanne, his sister's features in him. He wasn't looking at me, his weakened eyes were lost in the sky, through the open window. He looked like he had waited for this moment for a long time, as if he had been waiting for the release of a film at the cinema for several months and was determined to enjoy it as much as he could. So, I was responsible for not disappointing him. He knew the book, so if he was disappointed, it could only be because of my reading. After this brief glance, I didn't look at him anymore, concentrating on the story.

A few minutes later, perhaps quarter of an hour later, as I reached the end of the first chapter, I lifted my head slightly to see if there would be a reaction. But there hadn't been any change in the attitude of my landlord, who was listening, almost religiously. Interpreting his silence as an encouragement, I continued without interruption. At five o'clock forty five precisely, at the end of a sentence of the fourth chapter, Rodolphe Pardon suddenly seemed to wake up.

- It's time to stop. We'll go back to it on Tuesday evening at seven forty five, just after diner. Thank you.

And he stood up without waiting for any answer, as if he was firmly ending the session. I stammered a vague "thank you, too" and got up to put the book on a coffee table, leaving at the last read page a blue piece of ribbon I found there, just a little thing as solitary as me in this moment. A bit confused by the hasty attitude of my listener, I went back to my things.

So did it go on for each session - that is to say, four times a week, on Sunday, Tuesday, Thursday and Saturday. Always the same ritual, always exactly the same amount of time, always at exactly the same place. My host would end the reading almost brutally every time, sticking to his precision and punctuality. I didn't get offended anymore, I had gotten used to it and it suited me, and it was now part of my new life environment. Indeed, I appreciated these sessions, which represented a relaxing break in my hard daily studies. The exercise, as I had noticed, helped me to clear my mind, or even inspired me in my studies. I sometimes looked forward to the reading time with as much impatience as my partner. However, he never changed the time, even when we both were available long before. We always started exactly at the right time, not even a minute later.

The story of Jean and the widow Couderc fascinated me. I could feel the end would be tragic as the atmosphere grew more and more heavy, but the author was leading us slowly towards it, leaving us the time to imagine all kinds of drama between the boorish yet so passionately human characters. Since the book wasn't very long, we moved on quite quickly to a famous book I knew and appreciated, The Lady of the Camellias, then another, Froth on the Daydream by Boris Vian. I did my best to adapt to these totally different universes, desiring to do well. My landlord still hadn't expressed his feelings about the quality of my reading, so I just had to guess. It happened that, during weekends when we were having lunch with Jeanne, she would ask me which story we were reading. Rodolphe Pardon answered by saying the title of the book, but giving no more details. One day, as I was helping his sister in the kitchen, she told me he was very happy with me. I shouldn't take offence if he wasn't saying anything about it, as he wasn't the kind of man to express his satisfaction. At last, thanks to this confession, I felt better, relieved and it allowed me to see beyond the straight laced personality of my listener. Feeling encouraged, I was enjoying the sessions more, trying to dress up nicely too, and to sit in a posture that would perfectly orientate my voice towards him… In this way, we made a ritual of literature.

Outside of these special moments, I didn't have a minute for me. I was totally immersing myself in my researches and studies, aiming to be improving every day, discovering a new artist, contacting someone from the art field, understanding artistic trends in other countries… I wanted to know everything possible. Our teacher reminded us that we had to do a three day internship at a professional artistic company. I was happy to hear during a call that the art salesperson who Marc had introduced me to the year before, perfectly remembered my application, and me too at the same time. The internship, during which I had received a lot of flattering references to the professional quality service of my former landlord, happened to be a boon for meeting new people and I took advantage of it, asking seemingly thousands of questions and writing down everything that could be useful. This urge to learn, I'm sure of it now, was fed, even provoked by the fact that I was far away from home, and at the same time by the numerous opportunities of the city. But also by the reading sessions, which gave my schedule a rhythm, punctuating my study periods like refreshing breaks, allowing me to recharge my batteries. I didn't quite miss my family, even if I was often thinking of them. I regularly called Greg and my family who were waiting to see me for a short holiday in October. They had a lot of things to show me for the wedding preparation, so I had to expect family meetings on this topic.

Just before the holidays, I had to do a research project about the balance of volume in sculptures from the classical period. I had planned to contact a specialist of this period Marc had presented to me the year before, from whom I preciously had kept the name and address because I didn't want to do an academic research. I wanted to present a personal and documented reflection on this topic. This contact, an old auctioneer, was now retired, but he didn't hesitate to let his friends and former colleagues benefit from his knowledge, just for the love of art. Indeed, he had kept his former office to receive visitors. Marc and I had eaten with him one day and that had been an unforgettable experience for me as the man had made such a big impression on me. He had had memorable sales, some of which were mentioned as references in the most elite fields. Could I get in touch with him directly or should I ask Marc first? It would be an opportunity to know how he's doing, perhaps even to see him again. But what if he didn't want to? Perhaps he had turned over a new leaf with the memory of our relationship? He had never tried to reach me, or even left the slightest message. I should perhaps then understand that I shouldn't try anything either. After all that we had experienced together… No, I was very naïve to think like that, because for him, it was just another adventure, whereas for me… Well, better not to think about it anymore.

Daniel Montel, the auctioneer, needed a few seconds to remember me over the phone. He seemed to have to search in his memory, because our meeting happened more than nine months ago.

- Wait, I have it, I got it. Marc has so many work partners, I was mistaking you for his development manager. Of course, I remember you very clearly now, you were so reserved at first, though you were much more relaxed by the end of the meal. How are you doing? Are you still in Paris? If I remember well, you come from the south of France, don't you?

I confirmed to Mr. Montel that I was still studying in Paris, and I actually had some questions to ask him about a certain topic. I explained the context of my research and how he might be able to help. It was about helping me to orientate my research on classical artists, who were the most concerned by the topic of volume in sculpture. Immediately, he seemed excited.

- But it's really fascinating! I could actually bring you some ideas, or at least, possible directions for your research. What do you think about coming to my office this week? I would be delighted, I owe a lot to Marc, a real decent man, and I would be glad to help one of his dearest friends.

One of his dearest friends? I was one of Marc's dearest friends? Did he mechanically say that or had Marc confessed this fact while speaking about me? I didn't have time to ask - Mr. Montel already had hung up.

We had agreed to meet in two days at half past six, at the other end of the city. Luckily, it wasn't a reading day and I just let Rodolphe Pardon know I would come back home later than usual. He offered to keep a plate of food warm for me.

On the day, holding my research file, I rang at Mr. Montel's molded and varnished office door. I was a few minutes late due to a poor timing of metro connections. Luckily, he didn't seem to be offended. Not everybody was as punctual as my landlord. At the moment, Mr. Montel was talking to a young woman who was obviously ready to leave.

- Laura, here is Sonia Faure. She's a great artist, a wonderful sculptor. Sonia, this is Laura, a friend of Marc. She studies Arts. Are you sure you have to leave, Sonia?
- Yes, I have a meeting, thanks Daniel, for all your advice. Laura? Your name seems familiar to me… You've lived at Marc's place, have you? I just had dinner with him last week.
- Oh! Is he alright?
- … Yes, very well. Haven't you seen him for a long time?
- Well, no, actually, not for several months.
- Oh? Call him, then, he'll be happy. Anyway, I better be leaving now. Have a good evening!

I would have liked to ask more questions, to know if Marc had a new student, if he had talked about me, if he had told her he would like to receive a call from me. All these people who were in contact with him seemed to know me a little bit, as if Marc had told them about our relationship - or was it just my imagination? And this Sonia, did she also have special relationships with him? I was a little bit frustrated, aching to know more.

After having escorted his friend out of his office, Mr. Montel invited me to sit in a little corner close to a window overlooking the courtyard.

- Would you like a glass of wine?

Marc's friends were clearly like him, particularly welcoming. I was a little bit cautious, but this man didn't seem to expect anything else from me, or as if he were trying to seduce me. He looked very serious. While tasting the glass of Bordeaux, which immediately made me relax, we started to talk about the topic I had chosen. There again, my host seemed to know all about the period concerned, and well able to suggest numerous ideas. I made note of them, writing them down carefully in my school exercise book, aware of the value the knowledge this man was sharing with me, as the passionate professional who had devoted his life to art. Almost two hours passed by like that, without me noticing, being so absorbed in my speaker's discourse. I had collected more research material than I could have possibly hoped for.

Mr. Montel finally stopped speaking, also starting to become aware of time spent. Breathing out, he settled in his armchair and looked at me.

- My wife and I have invited some friends for
dinner tonight. What do you think about joining
us? We'll find someone to drive you home.

As we were driving to his place, I called Rodolphe
Pardon to let him know I, as an exception, would be
having dinner away from home. He didn't seem
surprised and hung up, not before wishing me a good
evening. Mr. Montel, who had overheard the
conversation, briefly continued the discussion.

- Are you living at a relative's place?
- No, I'm renting a room at an old mans' place in
  exchange for taking time to read to him.
- Really ?
- Yes, it's a service exchange.
- I understand. That's very clever. I also was
  sharing my apartment when I was a young
  student. My family was in Brittany, it's a bit far
  away. Six years studying in Paris, it comes out
  to be pretty expensive.
- I just have two years, but already it's a heavy
  budget. Luckily, I've found this solution for a
  room to stay in.

I thought he was going to speak about Marc, asking me what kind of service I had given him in exchange for the room, because he sure had heard the sculptor say I had lived with him, but he didn't add anything. Once again, I had the impression he was avoiding the subject, and I remained frustrated.

The auctioneer's apartment was like what I imagine it could be: full of rare and precious objects - a little bit too much perhaps, a real treasure cave. I was ecstatic in front of the bronze sculptures and paintings displayed in the vast entry hall.

- You know, these, they're just one part of my collection. The most precious ones are in a safe place. I couldn't simply leave them here. Unfortunately, it's impossible to enjoy the most beautiful pieces day to day! Come on, I'm going to introduce you to the others.

It was a little after half past eight and most of the guests, about ten people, were gathered in a little lounge where they were having a drink with the company of Mrs. Montel. There were two painters, a sculptor, two lawyers among whom I recognized the one I had met at Marc's office and who seemed to remember me, an opera singer, a writer, a notary, a collector and a business woman. I was like a bird fallen out of the nest in amongst these professionals, but when Mr. Montel presented me as Marc's friend, everybody came to shake my hand, as if just saying this name meant I was part of the group, as if I was one of them. I was touched by that, though I don't know why. Perhaps because they represented everything I desired, the reason why I was working so hard. I would have liked to tell them about my admiration, my hopes, but that would probably have seemed naïve and out of place, so I made my best to follow the discussions, while trying to remember name and profession of each person. I would write them down in my notebook as soon as I got back home.

Mrs. Montel was charming, dinner was pleasant, even if I almost ate nothing. I was too excited, too alert for my throat not to be tight. The singer came closer to me, as we were getting up from the table.

- What a pity Marc couldn't make it tonight, don't you think?
- Was he invited?
- Of course, Marc is always invited!
- Do you know him well?

- Quite well, yes. We often see each other at friends' places when I'm in Paris. I like him a lot.

So that was where Marc was spending his evenings, but where did he spend the rest of his nights?

At that moment, the writer interrupted us.

- I was told to take you back home. I live in your quarter, so we'll take off when you're ready - I'm at your service!

CHAPTER XIII

As the novelist opened the door of his car for me, after having thanked and said goodbye to all the guests, I began to boil inside. Answering my question, as he drove through the city, he recounted to me the origin of his last book - a story about families fighting for the acquisition of a famous hotel, but who end up demolishing the hotel, after having come together to operate it, because they discovered an ancient site under the building, while working on the foundations. I did my best to follow the steps of this tortuous story but my mind was agitated. The novelist went on and on, not noticing anything about my state of agitation.

- … But she didn't want to believe it, you see, because Lucie's father was a violent man and she didn't want her son to suffer as she had…

Marc said he liked this story very much - did he ever talk about it with you?

In reality, I had eaten very little and drunk much more than usual. And I had been constantly been on my toes throughout the evening, trying to appear confident and follow multiple conversations, and feeling a little annoyed by people mentioning Marc's habits, Marc's qualities, Marc's unusual absence… I was just looking forward to resting my mind and body.

I left my chauffeur for the evening, thanking him and accepting his business card, and hurried up to the apartment, careful not to wake up my landlord at this late hour. It was past two o'clock in the morning and I had to get up at seven for school.

Once in bed, I couldn't fall asleep. I had had a very good evening, I had collected information I needed, met a lot of interesting people… However, I couldn't relax now. I didn't understand this mystery about Marc, these indirect references to our relationship - I had questions for everything. If he had talked about me to these people, what did he say? And if that was the case, why did they all seem to keep it almost as a mystery? And, I admit, I felt a little bit jealous. Marc really knew a lot of people, as many women as men, and I had no idea of the kind of relationship they had with him, particularly in the intimate, sexual sphere. If all or some of these women had shared a relationship with him, whatever the kind, did they know it was also the same for me? When they were talking to me about him, should I have understood any double meanings? I felt lost.

The next day, when my alarm rang after an agitated night, I jumped out of bed and ran into the shower. Warm water, then cold, helped me clear my mind. After having gotten dressed, I prepared myself a strong and hot coffee, and took a few minutes to think. So, looking back, I now had the impression I had exaggerated a lot about the situation at last night's dinner. It probably was the excited atmosphere which had made me go crazy, as much as the pressure I had imposed upon myself to be like the others. This special world was so sparkling, so alive… But I quickly had to return to my studies, because I was still just a simple student. I had a degree to work towards and I was engaged, almost married - my life was with Greg. As I finally made my way to the apartment's door, ready to start my school day, Rodolphe Pardon appeared in a dressing gown at the end of the corridor.

- Laura, did everything go well? I heard you coming back very late, I was a little worried.
- Everything's alright, thank you for your concern. But now I have to leave, so we'll see each other tonight for reading, won't we?
- Of course, as usual.

I came back on time for dinner, seven o'clock precisely, after a busy and productive day, despite feeling tired. The table was set and the meal, cooked by Jeanne, was warming up. Rodolphe Pardon was busy around the stove.

- Laura, can I ask you to turn up the heat under the pot, please? I can't see this kind of detail very well, even with glasses.
- Of course, like that, is that okay?
- A little more, I think, the broth has to simmer a little.
- Okay, just a little bit more, there you go. I think that's good.
- It'll be ready in a minute. In the meantime, let's pour ourselves a glass of wine, shall we?
- Just a small glass, thanks.

I didn't really want to have any wine, after last night's party, but I joined my dining partner. I felt he wanted to talk, which was a change from our daily routine.

- I still haven't had the opportunity to tell you, Laura, but I'm very satisfied with our routine. You're discreet, careful, on time, and I like the way you read.

I didn't really know what to say. Mr. Pardon was an intimidating, difficult to understand man, and these few words sounded to me like an official declaration, something of real value. Responding, I was afraid to say too much or too little.

- Thank you, Sir. It's the first time I've done such a thing, but it's a real pleasure to read for someone. I would never have guessed how much I enjoy it.

He slightly smiled. I did think it was the first time I saw him smiling and it suited him very well, he was looking less distant. I wanted to ask him if I could call him by his surname but he quickly got up to take the pot off the stove.

- One minute precisely, at low temperature. It's almost ready!

After dinner, we got ready for reading. After Alexandre Dumas, we had moved on to Françoise Sagan with *Bonjour Tristesse* (Hello Sadness). I now just had to go with flow of the story, sitting comfortably in my usual spot. I seemed to notice a change slowly taking place in the room, without finding precisely what it was. At the end of the reading, I couldn't resist asking the question.

- Yes, I've changed all the bulbs. I couldn't see well enough. It's better now.

I felt sorry for this man, whose pride seemed affected. It might have been difficult for him to admit he was more and more dependent on others, but I couldn't do anything else than the reading, the reason he had let me enter into his life. He wouldn't have liked me to offer him help for any other task, only if he were to ask me himself.

I spent the rest of the evening studying, as the research I had to do was due at the end of the week, and meanwhile I was still hoping to meet a museum director who was having an exhibition of contemporary sculpture. I was thinking of adding this reference to my research. Then, I was going to go to Biarritz for six days. The week's program didn't give me time to think of anything else. I had to go on with my studies, memorising knowledge. Unfortunately, the museum's director proved unreachable. An assistant was covering him and despite my repeated calls, the answer remained the same.

"Sorry, Mr. Chairman is at a meeting. He can't answer your call, please, try again later."

I was very annoyed because I had a lot of expectations for this appointment which should have helped me to integrate an important element in my conclusions. I would just have to do without it – well, except if... yes, I now knew painters, sculptors and a collector, who all had been there at the auctioneer's place, and surely one of them could help me obtain this appointment at the museum.

The next evening, I took my notebook in which I had carefully listed all the people I had met since the previous year, with their name, profession, date, place of the meeting and, if possible, their phone number. I prepared my little monologue and started with the sculptor.

"Hello Mr. Denys, I'm Laura, a friend of Marc's. We recently met at Daniel Montel's party. I would like to know if you could do me favour…"

Monsieur Denys was charming. He promised to call the museum's director himself to try to quickly get me an appointment. He had already been in contact with this museum and he thought he could help me. I thanked him and hung up, congratulating myself for handling this like a professional, and was already imagining myself as one. Meanwhile, I had asked him where his own exhibition was being held, so that I could visit and admire his masterpieces. Now, I could continue my research and, the sculptor having fulfilled his promise, I was able to hand in a completed and original project, on time, to my research director.

Already, the station platform. Already, the departure. Time was flying by. It was October already, and I was thinking about what I had to do at school upon my return. I studied during almost the whole journey, contemplating my future projects, recapping knowledge I had learned so far, making a list of exhibitions I wanted to see. There was so much to discover, so much to know.

When I arrived in Biarritz, it was a completely different atmosphere. From a study environment, I jumped into the excitement of the family. Hugs, kisses, everything was bringing me back to expansive family affection, whereas at the moment I was just a productive study machine. I adapted myself to it, with some regret, but I ended up enjoying being with them.

Greg was still so careful. He was attentive and full of and tenderness. He offered me flowers and took me out for dinner…

- You know, I had an interview for a job helping with the town's sport activities, and according to Martine, the town council's secretary, I'm almost sure to get the job! That'd be fantastic, wouldn't it? We could quickly rent an apartment thanks to my pay! And then, come, I want to show you the suits I have picked out for our wedding. You tell me which one you prefer.

I barely answered. I never had the time to express myself before another project, another idea was presented to me, from one member of the family or another. It never seemed to stop, during the first four days of holiday. Living in Paris in an organised, studious and hard-working environment, I couldn't follow this profusion of emotions and excitement all around me. Nor could I understand where the uneasy sensation I felt inside of me was coming from, among those who wanted my happiness so much. I ended up feeling annoyed by all this concern about a topic which should have been my own priority, my own big event. The day before leaving, as Greg, for what seemed like the thousandth time, was suggesting to me yet another possible bloody flower arrangement to decorate the wedding, I shouted at Greg and all the family, exasperated:

- I would like you to leave me in peace! I don't want to get married, I want to be free to choose my own life!

I pronounced these words with such firmness and in such a sudden way that all the room's enthusiasm evaporated on the spot. I was hearing myself throwing out everything I had kept in my heart for several months, as if I was another person. I saw Greg cycle through several expressions in quick succession. At first he smiled slightly, as if he thought I was joking, then surprise appeared on his face when he understood I was serious. Finally, his eyes were showed doubt, before crashing into worry. All this in a few short seconds, as I was staring at him without blinking a single time, surprised by the harshness of my own words and unable to add anything else. The other members of the family who were there were swinging their eyes from Greg to me, astonished and stunned. They seemed to be wondering if I was going crazy. Greg's mum was the first to react, after a few seconds.

- Are you tired, Laura? Are you alright?
- No, I'm not alright. You're all very nice but I don't want to get married.

Greg, shocked by these few words of mine, seemed to get a grip on himself, if with difficulty.

- You don't want to marry me, is that what you said?
- No, I don't want to get married at all. It's not because of you.
- But why didn't you say it earlier?
- I don't know. I tried, I didn't dare, I wasn't sure. You all looked like so happy about it, I didn't want to disappoint you.

Only my father seemed to get over the emotion.

- I understand, my dear. We've insisted too much, you're right. We have to listen to what's important for you. Come, let's leave them together - they need to talk alone.

CHAPTER XIV

Explaining to my fiancé that the wedding, planned for a few months later and long expected, wouldn't take place, was something I ought to have prepared in advance, rather than expressed in the moment with everybody around. The simplest words hurt whatever the way they were expressed.

- I think it's the idea of getting married I'm not feeling okay with. It doesn't feel right. It seems too restrictive, and that's troubling me.
- It's too restrictive to marry me? Well, I didn't know you're thinking these kinds of things. For me, it was a joy to know we were getting married.

- Don't take it personally, it's nothing against you. It would be the same with anybody else. I simply am not ready for it.
- Anybody else? I'm not just anybody else! I already felt something was different since your departure to Paris last year - you weren't the same anymore with me. But I thought it was because of the change of environment, the distance, and that had disturbed you for a while. Now, I think it's more serious than that. Have you met someone else?
- No, not at all.
- So why have you been so much less intimate with me? You're distant, insensitive, not like you were before.
- Oh, really? I don't know, I haven't noticed.
- I think it's better not to talk about it for now. You don't seem to understand what I'm saying.
- Greg…

It was impossible to keep the discussion going. He had already left his parents' house, where we had been visiting. I found myself alone in the room, offended. He was right, I knew well I wasn't behaving with him like before, but I didn't want to face reality and he had been bearing it for several months without talking to me about it, even though he might have suffered because of it. I felt awful, I had hurt him and he was unhappy. It made me feel sad. But at the same time, paradoxically, I felt relieved. For more than a year, I had been playing a game. I wasn't in love anymore, and it seemed obvious now that I had to open up about it and be honest. It was as if talking about it had allowed me to become more conscious of it, for sure. As I was pronouncing the words, I had felt it vividly, that it was really what I meant. Indeed, I had spoken without thinking, without preparing anything. It had come out without me wanting it, as if it couldn't stay inside of me anymore. I should have done it earlier but it had seemed so difficult to destroy everybody's hopes, to shatter their expectations for me.

I came out through the rear door, finding Greg's parents and mine in the garden. They were walking around or sitting, waiting with a concerned look on their faces. Greg had gone through the front door, probably to escape from them, in order not to have to explain to them what he himself couldn't accept. When I appeared, they lifted their heads altogether. I could read in their eyes they were questioning me and waiting for a positive ending, a legitimate explanation, even though they didn't dare to hope for it. I took a breath.

- Greg's gone. I'm sorry, I've explained to him the wedding seemed too soon for me, but now he's annoyed with me. I didn't want to hurt you all, I'm sorry.
- Come on, it's not the end of the world, my dear. It'll be alright. These things happen. Getting married can scare people, especially at your age. Come, don't worry.

I ran into my dad's arms and fell into tears. The emotion reached Greg's parents, who cried too, and my mum who held back her tears with difficulty.

- Let's go home now. Greg surely will be back soon and he would probably like to be alone with his parents.

We took off, leaving Greg's mum and dad speechless and lost, standing in the garden, where they didn't seem to want to move. The way back home was silent because there was nothing to say about what had happened. It now only concerned Greg and me. From time to time, my mum gazed at me with eyes full of tenderness and understanding as if she was trying to reassure me, like the day when I had broken my ankle as a child, and was taken to the hospital. After a quick dinner, I took refuge in the little hut in the garden. It was cold inside, but I needed space to think too. There were Greg's things, his books, his sports shoes, a razor, his toothbrush. He hadn't called, I had no news from him. My parents had called his home, and though he was back he didn't want to talk to me for the moment. I lay down on the large bed we had shared so many times together and covered myself with the old wool blanket. Perhaps our story wasn't over, perhaps were we going to get together again, to be like before… I ended up falling asleep.

I woke up at dawn, waking to a cool and rainy morning, alone. The sound of rain drops on the wooden roof reminded me of my childhood, when I used to listen to the same sound in my bedroom, dreaming of the future. I stayed around ten minutes like that, without moving, wrapped in my blanket. It was my departure day, and my future dreams were becoming more precise. They were more concrete than when I was a kid, and it seemed that Greg wasn't part of them. Nevertheless, I was feeling good. I had a quick look at my cellphone - no message. He still hadn't digested the shock. I got up and entered the family house. Everybody was still asleep at this early hour. I prepared myself a cup of coffee and a couple of slices of toast. I was hungry, though I felt a little ashamed that I didn't feel worse after what had happened. My mood was almost joyful, actually. I had only said what I was feeling in my heart, I had talked honestly. What could I have done better under these circumstances? If we weren't going to stay together, Greg would find happiness with another girl, without any doubt. I ate my toast, enjoying the crusty taste of the bread and the softness of fresh butter, and then started to prepare my things for the departure which was planned for eleven twenty. I suddenly remembered it was Greg who was going to take me to the station. Of course, he wouldn't do it, so I would ask his parents. Another quick look at my cellphone, still nothing. I decided to call. If Greg didn't want to take me, we at least had to communicate, to show we still respected one another. I dialled his number, it was now half past eight, he answered.

- Hi, Greg? It's Laura.
- Yes, I know.
- Are you feeling okay?
- No, I'm not. I haven't slept all night.
- Are you angry with me?
- Yes, a bit. But I think I knew it would happen like this. You're so different. I don't recognise you anymore.

- Listen, Greg, let's give it some time. I will come back for Christmas and we'll see then what we'll do. What do you think?
- If you want. Anyway, I'll come to take you later to take you to the station, as planned.
- Are you sure?
- Yes, we're not going to leave each other like that.

Later, together in the car, unease saturated the atmosphere. Greg, feeling as uncomfortable as me, turned on the radio to fill the silence, but nothing helped.

- You've never told me much about your Parisian life, Laura. Since you left last year, I hadn't known much at all, and I probably haven't been curious enough. I guess some things are difficult to make up for.
- Yes, I understand, Greg. But it's not your fault.

Arriving at the train station, he helped me to take my luggage out of the car and kissed me on the cheek.

- Take care.
- See you soon, Greg. See you at Christmas.
- Christmas it is.

It was hard to leave, seeing him in such a bitter mood. I would have liked to reassure him, to tell him everything was going to be like before, but I couldn't. Once more, I got onto the train, heading in the direction of my second life, the one I was the only one to know, the one that had chosen me. I should have talked to Greg, letting him know what had happened there in Paris, the people, my relationship with Marc, my ambitions, my discoveries about myself, about others. He could have understood, at the very least he would have more of an idea. Why hadn't I said anything all this time? Why did I make as if my life in Paris was out of time and didn't concern the one waiting for me in Biarritz? I believed my Parisian life would end at the same time as my degree but I was wrong. I was wrong because I didn't want that, I wanted it to continue, I wanted more of it.

Having been so deep in my own thoughts, I instead dived enthusiastically back into my study and research for the rest of the journey. This way, I wasn't thinking about my sad and dying love story anymore. When I arrived at the apartment, several hours had passed and I almost felt dizzy from everything I had been working on in the train. Rodolphe Pardon welcomed me as warmly as possible.

- Hello Laura, good to see you. I need a reading session, you know. I got awfully bored being alone here. I've picked out all sorts of books.
Oh, by the way, there's a message for you. I left the note on the chest of drawers by the door. It's Jeanne who received the call yesterday at midday, as I was in the bathroom. She has written down everything for you. But come now and eat, there's a gratin waiting.

The message was from Marc. Just a few words.

"You've made a very good impression on my friends at Daniel Montel's party. Bravo!"

Nothing more. Not a hello, nor a "how are you doing?" Nothing. What was I supposed to think of this message? That he hadn't forgotten about me? That he wanted to see me? Or simply that they had talked about me and at that time, he had wanted to briefly show himself through a little note? Should I call him? I didn't know. I wanted to - I would have liked to see him again, at least just to meet for lunch. But at the same time, I wondered if it was the right time, just after having called off my wedding with Greg. I then remembered the sculptor's words at Daniel Montel's place.

"You should call him, he would be very glad."

I couldn't forget this sentence, among other comments from Marc's friends. They were carved in my mind as hopeful promises to see him again. Now that I was emotionally free, I could think about seeing him again, if he wanted to. Nothing was holding me back anymore. Keeping this idea in my mind, I fell asleep that night with thoughts of my former partner.

The following week was exhausting. Greg tried to call me several times until I found the time to call him back, on Wednesday evening. He wanted to know what I was feeling, if I felt regretful, if I really wanted to cancel the wedding - because they already had made a down payment for the reservation of the room.

- I'm sorry, Greg, I won't go back on my decision. I'll pay that down payment, don't worry.
- It's not a question of money, but what should I say to everybody?
- Tell them we were too fast, but our senses came back to us, and now we'd prefer to wait before we settle down, or something like that.
- So are you really sure?
- Yes, I'm sure.

This conversation took place in the corridor. I didn't bother to go into my bedroom. I wasn't used to hiding myself away and often left my door open, except when I was take a shower or getting changed. I hadn't noticed Rodolphe Pardon was just next to me, in the lounge. He had overheard everything, and when I hung up, I saw him looking at me.

- Everything's alright, Laura ?
- Yes, very well, Mr. Pardon. It's a personal matter.

He seemed to wait for more details and I decided to talk to this man I lived with, shared dinners with, and read to.

- I was going to get married, but I called it off just a few days ago. My fiancé hasn't taken it so well, and he wanted to be sure I didn't act on an impulse.
- Well, indeed, you're more menacing than you look. I wouldn't want to be in his place, in any case! It might be difficult to accept such a thing. Especially coming from a charming young woman like you.
- Thanks. Yes, it's difficult for the family too. But they'll get over it.
- Okay, if you're feeling well anyway, I'm going to go to bed. My eyes feel a bit tired – a sure sign I should be going to bed. Good night!
- Good night to you too.
- Oh, while I'm thinking about it, could you put an envelope in the caretaker's letterbox tomorrow morning, on your way out? It'll help me to avoid having go down myself. You see, my sister wants me to go out alone as little as possible. She says I might have an accident at any moment because of my bad eyes. She's exaggerating, but all the same.
- Of course, I'll do it. You can count on me.

-   Thanks, Laura.

This conversation didn't go any further. Yet, I had the impression that as strange flatmates Rodolphe Pardon and I were, we had made a big step forward. I was very happy about it, because I was starting to find this man much more interesting than I had imagined him to be.

CHAPTER XV

My feeling grew to be confirmed over days and weeks which followed. As I got back into my study routine and Christmas was getting closer, my landlord was becoming more and more friendly, though without going beyond his own limits. But we were starting from so little, that just a short, personal sentence had the value of a treasure. I was enjoying these brief personal moments. They gave me a feeling of a familial atmosphere.

- Laura, come here, I've been able to put the thread through the eye of the needle in one go! I have to mention that to Jeanne, she never stops worrying about me! It turns out I still can see well, actually!

M. Pardon was actually a very charming man, and I enjoyed reading for him as well as helping him daily – more and more often – with little tasks. Checking the water meter, recounting the money put aside for the firemens' New Year's present, reading the new instructions from the building union - all that had become difficult for him and, without really noticing, I managed to be around as often as possible every time he needed help.

I was thinking of my life with Marc, our wild evenings, the nights spent on the sofa, the evenings out until early morning… a crazy life, the opposite of the one I was sharing with Rodolphe Pardon. However, there were some common things between the two men who otherwise seemed so separate. It was their way of saying things, how they listened carefully before giving an opinion, a certain perspective on life… they sometimes even used the same words, or somewhat old-fashioned expressions like "it's not my cup of tea" or "don't sell me a dog".

I had imagined calling Marc a hundred times since my return from Biarritz. I sometimes dreamed of having his eyes on me, his presence close to me. Even still, I had stopped myself, being afraid of his reaction. If I was wrong, and he didn't want to see me again at all, that would be too much for me. In that case, I would be the one abandoned, the one left behind and I didn't want to take the risk at that time.

I needed all my optimism to finish my year of study in the best conditions and to gather all the advantages on my side. It wasn't courageous but I had put too much effort to just take the risk to spoil everything.

Time passed by, at the pace of the books I read.

The one day, when coming back from school a little later than usual, I didn't find my landlord at home in the apartment. It was very strange. The only other time it had happened, he had left me a note to let me know he would be back later. But now, after having looked everywhere, on the kitchen table and on the pinboard, in the lounge and even in my bedroom, but there wasn't any message. I knocked on his bedroom door and opened it slightly to see if he was taking a nap, but it was empty. There was no trace of him. The apartment was exactly as usual, but without him. At this hour, where could he be? Then, I thought he might have gone out to see someone in the building, perhaps the caretaker, and he would be back in a moment. So, I waited, but after three quarters of an hour, I couldn't stand it anymore and called Jeanne, who had given me her phone number. A man answered, but I didn't recognize my landlord's voice.

- Hello, I'm Laura, could I talk to Jeanne, please?
- Hi, I'm Jeanne's husband. She's not here. She's received a call from the hospital saying her brother had had a fall in the street, so she's over there with him.
- Is it serious? Did he fall on his head?
- I don't know much more. It might have happened late afternoon and some people called the firemen. Jeanne left about an hour ago. I don't think she had time to call you - nor me, actually.
- Do you have the address of the hospital?
- Yes, I'll give it to you.

On the way, I was feeling worried for my daily companion. He was strong, yes, but I knew falling at his age could have serious consequences. I wondered if I should have been more careful, and if noticing that his eyes were getting tired was an sign I should have taken seriously and reported to Jeanne.

I arrived at the reception feeling a bit panicked, and asked to see Mr. Rodolphe Pardon. The receptionist answered that he was being looked after and I had to wait a little, though I could go upstairs and wait in the waiting room. I took a moment to drink some water and clear my mind. When I entered the waiting room, Jeanne was there, perched on the edge of an uncomfortable chair. She was surprised to see me. I went closer to say hello.

- Hi Jeanne, your husband let me know about the accident. What happened?
- He had a fall. He went out alone to buy bread, even though told him I would come to bring him some. He missed a step on the pavement and fell on his elbow. He broke his arm and has some bruising, but really it could have been worse, so we're lucky actually. But he'll have to stay here a few days as he can't come home with an arm in plaster, especially because he can't see very well. And he has to have regular checks to make sure his head is alright.
- Does it disturb you if I come to see him?
- No, on the contrary, it's very kind from you to have come so quickly. I was told to wait while he's being looked after, but if you want, you can go to see him as soon as it's possible. Come take a seat.

So both of us waited together, sitting next to one another in silence. There were several other people in the room waiting too. We could only hear the sound of breathing, coughing, whispering. It now was half past eight. The reading would have taken place at quarter to eight this evening, as usual on Thursdays, so we would have just finished.

Finally, someone came to tell us we could see him. I stood up, after an approving look from Jeanne, and followed the nurse to the bedroom. Rodolphe Pardon was lying there, on a bed too small for him, his arm wrapped in plaster and he was wearing a pair of pyjamas his sister might have brought for him. He smiled at me.

- Laura, you came all the way down here? You shouldn't have hurried yourself. It's nothing serious, just a broken arm. You'll have to stay alone at the apartment for few days. The doctor doesn't want me to leave before making sure everything's okay.
- No worries. But how are you feeling, does it hurt?
- Not really, actually. I'm a big boy, you know. But Jeanne was right, I must admit. I didn't see the step at all.
- I'm a relieved to see you're okay. I'm going to leave you to rest, and your sister would like to see you too. Would you like me to come back?
- Actually, I would like to ask you a favour, Laura.
- Yes?

- I think this hospital isn't too far away from your school. Would you be able to come by from time to time, before going home, to read to me here?
- Of course, if the visits are authorised late afternoon, I can come for our regular days, if you'd like.
- That would be wonderful. I won't be able to move a lot while I'm recovering, so your reading will be almost all the activity I get. Thanks, Laura.

Feeling relieved, I left Jeanne alone with her brother and went out, glad I could at least do something for him. He wasn't in danger and would be back at the apartment within a week or two at the most. He had asked me to bring Nausea from Jean-Paul Sartre, which we had already begun, for Saturday. Right now, I just had to go home. As I was leaving the hospital's parking lot, walking towards the metro, I saw a car drive by me and thought I recognised Marc. I turned to look, but the car was driving away towards the hospital's main entrance, a few hundred metres away, and the driver hadn't turned his head to look at me. Was I so obsessed with Marc that I was seeing him everywhere? The coincidence really would be extraordinary - why would he be here at this very moment?

The apartment seemed very empty to me, and I decided to go out again to do some shopping at the corner shop, which was open until late at night. Jeanne phoned me to confirm the doctors were optimistic and that she would bring my meals just as usual.

- Can I come to have lunch with you on Saturday, Laura?
- Of course, Jeanne, that would be very nice.
- Or actually, no, come to eat with us. I'll be glad to have you at home with us, and I'll be able to introduce you to my husband.
- Well, alright, sound great! See you on Saturday!

Jeanne lived a few metro stops away from her brother's place. Her apartment was quite modern, though smaller. She and her husband formed a harmonious couple. He was full of humour and she laughed a lot at his jokes. The meal was very relaxed, friendly and familial.

- So, you're going to visit this nice old Rodolphe later, Laura? He can't do without you now, what a success!
- Come on, Yann, stop annoying Laura, and serve us some coffee in the lounge, please!
- See, Laura, my wife still calls this little corner here a "lounge", where she has put a bench and a coffee table! She still hasn't understood our apartment isn't big enough for us to have a lounge!

Jeanne started laughing.

After coffee, I left my hosts, hugging them as I thanked them. I promised Jeanne I would call her in the evening after visiting her brother. She would be dropping by the next morning to bring me my meals for Sunday, but she really wanted to know about her brother already this evening, after the reading.

Reading to Rodolphe Pardon in the hospital room was a strange moment. Sitting on the comfortable armchair next to the bed, I felt as if I was taking on the role of nurse, as if reading to him could help to reduce the man's pain. Rodolphe Pardon was as alert as usual, not more so, nor less. He didn't seem affected by this place. His body wasn't moving except for his eyelashes, his eyes fixed overhead, staring at the ceiling. He interrupted me, as usual, after three quarters of an hour. I closed Nausea, with the blue ribbon as bookmark. He finally turned his eyes towards me and smiled.

-     Thanks, Laura. That was perfect.

We started our ritual again, just as it was back at the apartment, four times a week, in this place apart from the world. Words and sentences from more or less famous authors had taken on another dimension for me now, where nothing familiar surrounded us - not the furniture, not the carpets, or the decorations. I would jump straight into the stories, as they were the only element which belonged to us. And in order to feel better the moment, I drew from the book all that the environment couldn't provide. I let myself be completely by the story, drowned in the text, reading like I had never read before. I became the words, and I devoured them. I did all I could to make the story come to life for my one-man audience, who had become dependent on someone to read and now to walk too. I remember once, my state of mind a little more relaxed and flexible than usual, the situation of this temporarily handicapped man turned my senses upside down in a strange way: he was feeble and dependent, and I felt once more as if I was in the dominant position, such as I had been several months ago. For a few minutes, while I was reading, I saw myself again with Marc, and felt those emotions I had discovered with him during our intimate games. I don't know if Rodolphe Pardon felt disturbed by it as I read to him.

I made my way home alone, and again sat myself at my study desk, the research, analyses and report preparations I loved spread out before me. I knew more and more people in the artistic field, and made sure always to take the opportunity to contact one or the other, to meet them in a museum, an exhibition, a private viewing. I felt as if I were touching my dream.

Yet, aware of the fragile links with these people, I often called my parents, as well as trying to call Greg who didn't answer for several days. When he finally answered, he explained me he was thinking of doing an internship abroad, from January until April in Spain. He sounded well enough, and didn't speak about the cancelled wedding. We weren't imagining anything together anymore and only talked about the present. I talked to him about my courses, my researches and he told me about his sport successes, but something between us was broken and the relationship was forced into something new.

Christmas was coming closer and Rodolphe Pardon had been at the hospital for longer than expected. Finally, after three and a half weeks, he was authorised to leave the hospital. Jeanne took him home one day during the week and I had the happy surprise of finding him at home in the apartment after coming back from school. He came to greet me in the corridor.

- Here I am, fit again. It really is good to come back home. And to see you, at the same time!
- Thanks very much, and you too. It's great to see you back and on your feet! But, by the way, I have to remind you I'm leaving in two days to spend Christmas with my family.
- Yes, of course. Don't worry, Jeanne will come to visit me with her husband for a few days, to spend the holidays with me. It's a bigger apartment here, so it'll be perfectly comfortable.

In that case, I can leave without worry.

CHAPTER XVI

In Biarritz, everybody was preparing for the Christmas holidays and the town was looking bright and festive. Even though in Paris I had been able to admire even more spectacular decorations, it felt good to be back in the streets I knew well, where sometimes the same Christmas lights had been kept for years. Some quarters or public buildings didn't even take them down anymore, and instead they were simply turned off outside of the Christmas season, which had apparently become longer and longer, stretching now between October and February. I had arrived the day before, finding my parents waiting for me at the station, and my brothers and sisters too. Greg was spending Christmas with his family, as usual, but we had decided to catch up with each other the next day, in order to take stock of our relationship. Well, that was how I had expressed myself, without thinking too much, after Greg had asked me if I thought we should meet at all. That had confused me a little bit. I had bought him a present, in order to make up for the last Christmas when I had forgotten to bring him one. It was a beautiful small bronze sculpture I had kept in mind for a while and which I had managed to get for a cheaper price, thanks to a sculptor friend. In the afternoon, just as I was taking a moment to add a nice little note with the package, I had the surprise to receive a message from Marc. "Have a merry Christmas, Laura". Feeling touched, I hurried to answer him because I wanted him to know how I was pleased to receive his messages, even though they were rare and discreet. These few words, despite being perfectly ordinary, made me extremely happy and had me lose my mind. Even still, I didn't dare to express myself beyond reserved politeness. With all that suddenly in my mind, I forgot the little note for Greg.

Our Christmas Eve supper was very nice. My parents had put a lot of effort into it, as if they were showing me the wedding's cancellation couldn't spoil either daily life or a traditional family reunion. We didn't speak about the wedding, and nor had anybody made any reference to it since my return. It looked to me like a kind of familial agreement everyone was fulfilling. Nonetheless, to reassure everybody, I took a few minutes during the meal to tell them I was doing well, and I was keeping up my studies as well as ever. Though my brother, in answer to my positive attitude, thought it was a good idea to mention Greg.

- Greg, as far it seems, isn't doing so well. People say he's become withdrawn, reserved.
- How do you know that?
- His sister told me that. I saw her at the pharmacy.

Nobody added anything else, and dinner went on. Of course, I immediately felt concerned by the remark, as if there was a finger pointed at me. Greg's mood, normally always so positive, couldn't have been affected by anything else than our marriage being called off. He was such an optimist, such a joyful man. I hesitated to call him, to judge his state myself and try to clearly explain everything, because I couldn't stand feeling guilty towards him. In the end, the evening went on, and with the atmosphere and everybody's good mood I went to bed not thinking about it anymore.

The next day, I woke up around ten o'clock. I was going to meet Greg at eleven, having planned to head into town and meet at a nice little café, where we could speak quietly. I wasn't feeling very motivated, but I got dressed carefully, wanting to look good, put my hair back with a small silver hair-slide, and put Greg's present in my bag.

When I arrived at the café, he was already sitting at a table, an empty glass in front of him. I hadn't seen him for several weeks, but I immediately felt it wasn't necessary to speak. He had changed so much. His face looked serious, his eyes had lost their sparkle, he was sitting a little bit round-shouldered and it seemed to me his hair had become duller. I wasn't seeing him like before. I felt sure of it now, he wasn't the man of my life anymore. How do you know this kind of things? You just know it, that's all. You know when you have moved on. You don't see the other as having a part in your life any longer. It can't be explained, this feeling that is liberating but also weighs upon your conscience, because you feel the idea of separation is inevitable and is relieving, yet at the same time, you know you'll suffer. I forced myself with difficulty to present myself with a smile upon my face.

-   Hello Greg.
-   Hello. Do you want a drink?

The conversation was difficult to start. I sat there with a glass of apricot juice, staring across the table at Greg, who was trying to look better than he clearly felt. He too was trying to smile, he was trying to look relaxed, but his eyes looked suspicious and I was felt he was afraid of what I was going to tell

him. Sensing the need for direct honesty, I preferred
not to let the moment of doubt drag on any longer.

- I think it's better to break up.
- To break up? But why?
- Because it is what has already happened, and
it's better to make it clear.
- Really? We were already split up?
- I think so, yes. We're not together anymore.

He found it difficult to accept, but he did his best to
bear it and realise that my words marked a definitive
point of no return. We left the café to diffuse the
tension, walking along the main street. Greg offered
me to have lunch in a restaurant. I asked him if that
really was what he wanted, he answered no. He
preferred to have time alone.

I headed back home after this short *tête-à-tête*. There
was nothing more to say. I had even forgotten to give
him the small statue, finding it still in my bag as I
was looking for my day-pass to take bus back home.
I had clearly felt Greg had been disappointed, sad,
perhaps still hopeful, but I couldn't do anything
about it. When my parents saw me coming home so
early, they set another plate on the table and nobody
asked a single question.

Three days passed, during which I barely left home. I took time to enjoy my old habits with the family for a while, in the house I had known since childhood. I didn't go to the hut in the garden, which didn't have any interest for me without Greg, and one of my brothers, having asked me permission, took it for himself and his girlfriend. When I was watching them in each other's arms, I don't why, but instead of being reminded of my time with Greg, my time with Marc reappeared. He had thought of me during this Christmas break, he had found the time to write to me, even though he knew so many people and lived such a busy life. This fact filled me with joy.

I had to return to Paris on the fourth day, and didn't receive any call from Greg in the meantime. I didn't call him either. Our story was over.

In the train on the way to Paris, I made a decision. I had to meet Marc, I really wanted to see him again, I missed him. More than that, I *needed* to see him again. Tears came to my eyes when I was thinking of our time spent together - our laughs, our intimate secrets, our shared emotions. To make my life easier, I chose a deadline: if he hadn't called me before mid-January, I would call him myself.

At last, I arrived at the station. I was happy to see my landlord and my bedroom again. Both seemed to have waited for me. Rodolphe Pardon was looking very well. Enthusiastic as ever before, he told me about his Christmas meals with Jeanne and her husband and about the new books he had bought, some contemporary writers. I was as excited as him to discover all these new authors. I noticed that among them, two seemed to be more or less directly about sadomasochist relationship stories, or something similar. They would bring me back memories still fresh – in my mind, and in my heart.

Life started again as usual … Studying, reading, meetings with artists and others in the industry. My teachers encouraged me to continue to get in contact with people in the art world, to extend my net as much as possible. With several of my classmates, we used to share our contact lists once a week during a long lunch break. Each of us shared our good or bad experiences, meetings and projects, like a kind of big basket we held in common. This could be very interesting and save time for all of us. There was no competition between us. Instead, we supported and helped one another. We all knew we would find ourselves in the quite closed environment of art sales later.

One evening reading to Rodolphe Pardon, around the beginning of the second week of January, just as we ended our session he gave a gesture for me to stay sitting in my armchair and asked me to listen to him for a moment. Perhaps, I thought, he had something to tell me about his eyes or his health, so worrying a little I prepared myself to receive bad news.

- Laura, I have something to ask you.
- Of course, I'm listening. If I can be of any help…
- It's a little complicated. I would first like to let you know how much I appreciate your company. But you already know that.
- I appreciate yours as well - we're lucky!
- That's why I'm allowing myself to ask you… You'll see that I can only ask someone I entirely trust, but who's not from the family. Yet at the same time, someone who could well have been part of it, for you behave with me as with a close friend. I don't forget your presence at the hospital, or the fact that you're helping me with little details everyday…
- You make me want to know more! What is it about?

- About something that has meant a lot to me for years. It's a project I should have been busy with alone when my eyes were still good, though I never imagined they would become this bad. So, here we go: I dream of writing my biography, or actually, of having it written down, as I can't do it myself now. And I would like you to be the one to write it down.
- Me? But I'm not qualified, I'm not a writer!
- No need to be an author. What I need is someone who likes reading and writing, and above all, someone who's able to listen. Someone who knows me well enough, but not too much. And this… I know you can do it. You listen to my little complaints, my daily life, and you do it with patience. Of course, you would be paid for it.
- But when would we have enough time for that? It would take a while, it's a hard job.
- That's right, especially because I'd prefer to keep our reading time for the moment. I thought perhaps you could do it at the end of the year, during the summer holidays. What do you think? Two months of work. It should allow us to go faster, I haven't had such a busy life.
- Does Jeanne know about it?

- Of course, I talked to her about it. She also thinks you're the perfect writer. To be honest, she advised me to ask you.
- Really?
- Really, yes.
- I'll think about it, but I'm not sure I'm capable of doing it.
- Think about it, please do.

Later on in the evening, lying on my bed, I wondered to myself how come Jeanne and Rodolphe Pardon had thought that I would be the right one to write down his memoirs. The suggestion flattered me, but at the same time, I didn't know if I felt ready for such a job. I had never done much writing, and especially not to tell the story of someone's life. I really kept being surprised by my landlord, who at first seemed extremely reserved, and then all of a sudden wanted to reveal his whole life to a near-stranger. In any case, he had given me time to think it over, and I would really take it. I would give him my answer when I was confident, but not before.

Day by day, mid-January drew nearer, and thus, closer to the deadline I had chosen for myself regarding Marc. There was still no news from him, so I had to call him. One evening after reading time,

I made myself comfortable in my bedroom, sitting in my armchair next to the window. The apartment was quiet, my landlord was busy folding washing in the lounge. I took a breath. What would I say to Marc? I would say I had received his messages, which I had appreciated, that I had realised how much I missed him, and that I would like to see him. Oh God, it was a lot to say all that at once, but that was what I was feeling, so why beat around the bush and waste time? I always had thought thousands of couples on earth were never formed because of the fear of one of them to call and talk to the other one, and that that was a lot of missed happiness. I dialled the number, my heart beating like a crazy drum. Unfortunately, I was welcomed by the answering machine.

"This is Marc SOLIS's phone. I'm away right now, but leave a simple message and I'll call you back!

I hung up, disappointed. How could I say to an answering machine things that meant a lot for me? I preferred to call later. Suddenly, I was full of anxiety, and had to take a deep breath. Then I went to see my landlord.

- I'll help you fold these sheets.
- Thanks Laura. They're big, it'll be easier together.
- I've made my decision, about the biography.
- Really? That's great! I'm very happy about it.

Rodolphe Pardon really looked very happy with my decision. Delighted, he called his sister that same evening to let her know, and I could hear her enthusiasm bursting out from the phone. The project was in a way a family project, also concerning Jeanne since she always had been present in his life, and still was now. Both were obviously looking forward to this project, which for the time had only existed in my landlord's mind. For me, I still was surprised by all the enthusiasm. I had made my decision without really thinking about either the consequences or the difficulty of the task ahead of me. I needed to go with the flow I had been feeling since I had come back to Paris - trying, discovering, acting and not asking myself too many questions which could slow down my action.

- I'm going to think right now about how we'll organise ourselves. You see, you won't have to look after anything material. I'll be organising everything. Thanks a lot, Laura.

Before going to bed that evening, I decided to call Marc again. This time, he answered after just two rings. At the sound of his voice my chest tightened up instantly.

-   Laura? What a pleasant surprise! How are you?

His voice sounded so welcoming that I felt confused, though I hadn't forgotten the sentimental note I had left him before going. I explained to him plainly the purpose of my call, just as I had prepared it. I didn't want to give him time to discourage me.

-   Your messages, even if they've been rare since we last saw each other, made me realise how much I miss you. I really want to see you again.
-   Really? But, tell me, this sounds like a declaration of love, or have I understood it wrong?
-   Don't make fun of me. It's already difficult enough.
-   Shouldn't you soon be getting married?
-   I'm not getting married anymore. We broke up.

- Well then, let's have dinner together tomorrow evening, and you'll see I'm not making fun of you.

The next day wasn't a reading day, so I immediately accepted, despite all the study I had to get through. Nothing would prevent me to see him again.

CHAPTER XVII

The next day, all day long, I only thought of the coming dinner. I was completely absent during the commercial techniques class. My mind was away, my body alone was present. I wondered what I would be wearing, if Marc had planned a dinner at a restaurant or at his place, what would happen next… I dreamt of sharing an intimate moment with him just as we were used to, full of tenderness and love. My body wanted his so badly. Of course, I couldn't ignore his personality or his sexual tastes, but I didn't care. All that was a mere detail, and the pleasure of seeing him again was much stronger than the uncertainty about the lovemaking to come. Even if a genuine clairvoyant had foreseen the worst for me, I would have gone anyway, happy as a lark.

I ran into the apartment late afternoon, surprising and confusing my landlord. He knew I was meant to go out for the evening, but was surprised to see me suddenly so agitated. Usually he was telling everybody how quiet and reserved I was. I had left my last class in a hurry, paying no attention to my classmates, though we normally took some time to share ideas before heading home. Afraid of not having enough time to prepare myself as best as I could, I quickly stammered that I had an important appointment, and shut myself in my bedroom. Marc and I had planned to meet at half past eight in a café, a place I knew already, having been there once with my classmates. I was a simple and cosy place I had picked out, somewhere intimate, so I imagined, to facilitate the contact.

I put on my first choice of clothes with excitement, straight pants with a silk blouse, but a glance in the mirror made me change my mind. It looked too strict, and I already had worn it with Marc to go to one of his professional meetings. I quickly swapped it for a peacock blue dress with a light belt and heels. It looked much better, even if the soft material wasn't adapted to the season. To finish, I added a woollen coat. It was six forty-five, and I still had to take a shower, brush my hair and do my make-up before putting on the chosen dress. I couldn't waste any time, because the way to the café would take me around twenty-five minutes. I began to feel nervous, as I was scrubbing my long hair to dry them faster. I had to be quick to untangle this stock of hair, to rub the cream on my body, then to put a little bit of powder on my face, mascara, lipstick...

At last, I just had to put on my coat and I was ready. I quickly waved to say goodbye to Rodolphe Pardon without waiting for an answer, letting him know he shouldn't worry if I didn't come back that night, and left the apartment, not forgetting my brown handbag.

When I arrived at the café, though I was about ten minutes late, Marc still wasn't there. I took a quick walk around the block, because I didn't want to be the first one there and look like I was waiting for him. Approaching the café again, I saw Marc appear at the end of the street.

He was wearing a coat too, a sort of pea coat with rough canvas pants and Chelsea boots. I hadn't seen him wearing such clothes before, but they suited him very well and I immediately recognized his special charm. I ran into his arms, he held me tight against him.

- Wow, you're really happy to see me again!
- Marc, I'm so glad to see you!
- Let's come in. You're going to explain me all you've done since we left each other.

After having left the café, we went to a very nice, discreet restaurant. I didn't know what I was eating that evening. Rather, I was eating Marc's eyes, Marc's mouth, Marc's hands… I talked to him a lot, he listened a lot.

Then, we went to his place, very late, and we slept together, simply slept, it was a wonderful moment full of tenderness and intimacy.

In the morning, I slowly woke up, still in his arms. I had class, but this time I decided not to go to school for the day. I had better things to do. Marc opened his eyes too, while I still was enjoying the warmth of his body against mine. We made love as I had dreamed, with tenderness but also firmness, with determination and authority from him. The minutes following we spent as if floating on a cloud of happiness, of extreme fulfilment. I finally broke the moment, so that he wouldn't get up from bed.

- I'm the one preparing breakfast today. Will you lend me your kitchen?
- Okay, I'll stay in bed until you call me. Looks like things have changed!

That was true, something had changed. For the first time, our relationship seemed based on equality and he was allowing me to give him pleasure differently than belittling him.

Breakfast was ready after more than an hour of different kinds of more or less approximate preparations, as I courageously mixed French, English and American recipes from the most decadent breakfasts. I wanted it to be gargantuan, like the day I was hoping to spend with my lover, which would crazily swing between the kitchen and preferably the bedroom. Unfortunately, once we had finished eating, he announced to me he had to go.

-   Already? But I thought we would spend the whole day together! When are you coming back?
-   I'm leaving for six or seven months, to Asia.
-   What?
-   I have to travel to several countries in order to find development opportunities. This trip was planned two years ago. I didn't imagine you would decide to call me two days before my departure… But I didn't want to spoil our time together, which was wonderful. I'll be coming back at the end of summer, and then we'll have the whole life before us.

- I'll come with you.
- But you have to finish your studies, it's important. You're not going to give up on a whim. It'll go by fast, trust me. And we'll see each other at the end of summer.
- Seven months, that's a lot! I'm so disappointed.
- You shouldn't be. Waiting is sometimes the best moment, you know. I have waited for you a whole year long.

Marc had the way of presenting things nicely. I was sad to have to leave him after only a night, but I wanted to trust him and to keep the magic of our relationship going. And then, I had made a contract with Rodolphe Pardon for this summer, and I couldn't let him down, so I didn't really have the choice.

- Are you sure we're going to see each other again after you return?
- Of course! What could prevent from doing so? You're free now, aren't you? Me too.

Despite this bad news and the coming separation, everything seemed to make sense to me now. Marc was the man of my life. Certainly not the charming prince of my childhood stories, but the man who made me want to discover, to experiment, to live intensely. I kissed him.

- How much time do we still have?
- An hour. Precisely.

I went to the airport with Marc and we had a last hug full of emotion. We were close as ever before, even if we would be separated by thousands of kilometres. The plane took off and I watched it disappearing in the immensity of the sky, my face pressed against the window, my eyes fixed. Returning home and feeling exhausted, I sat at the terrace of a café, just by the stairs leading out of the metro. I spent the day dreaming, my head resting in my hand, or walking in a public garden, or down the street, looking at the shop windows without actually looking at them. I was wandering around, close to Rodolphe Pardon's quarter, wrapped into my woollen coat, still wearing my light dress and my patent leather heels. Marc had liked my dress a lot. I didn't want to go home yet, nor get changed. It was like I still was with him. My phone rang, it was my landlord.

- Excuse me, Laura, I couldn't stand waiting for news, so I decided to call you. I saw you hadn't come home yet, and your school had called here to check whether you were alright. I was worried.
- Sorry, I haven't let them know. Everything's okay, no worries. I had something else to do today. I'll call them back. Thanks, and don't worry, I'll be there later this afternoon for our reading.
- Great. See you later then, Laura.

The last few months of study were the hardest of all my semesters. I was doing my best to focus all my attention on my studies, keeping myself busy as much as I could in order to avoid thinking about my dear, recent memories, which were constantly threatening my concentration. I was studying very, very hard, and only left time free for the usual reading sessions. I was able to discover and appreciate the rich selection of books from my landlord, and enjoy new contemporary authors, detective novels, thrillers or philosophy books. At that time, Jeanne and Rodolphe were looking more and more excited about the biography project, gathering documents and photographs, remembering special moments or emotions which had come out thanks to the project. I tempered their enthusiasm a little, reminding them we had agreed on starting with a trial of a few days, and then confirm the project depending on how it goes.

-   But we're going to do everything for it to work properly, Laura. You would just have to listen and everything else will go fine.

Their trust touched me. I didn't dare to contradict them anymore.

From time to time, I received a call or a message from Marc. I suddenly left everything behind when that happened, no matter if I was at school in the middle of a course or dining with my landlord. He told me about people he met, and shared his disappointments. He already had obtained some results, though not enough to come back, as he said. Time passed by at the pace of these short discussions, because we both had a lot to do. However, I wasn't afraid of him leaving me anymore. He knew which words to say to reassure me and allow me to stay confident.

- You'll be able to move in with me as soon as I come back, Laura. I don't want to live without you anymore.

In April, I went to Biarritz for a few days for the Easter holidays. My parents found me radiant and nobody spoke about Greg, until my younger sister came to see me on the second day evening, looking embarrassed and kneading her fingers like a shy child.

- I have something to tell you. It's a little bit difficult to say.
- Really? What's up? Is it serious? Is it about our parents?
- No, not at all. It's about me, well, about us. Greg and me.
- Greg and you? What do you mean?
- We're together. We're going to get married.
- You're getting married to Greg?
- That's right.

For a moment, I thought she was joking, but seeing my sister's sheepish and uncertain face, I understood she was serious. Despite the extreme surprise caused by this sudden announcement, and a feeling of unpleasant infidelity, I didn't want to hurt her even more. I pulled myself together as quickly as I could.

- But that's very nice. I didn't know you were close friends.
- We weren't. Of course. But after you left, he came by to visit a few times. I think he needed to see us, to talk to us, to overcome his situation. He was very unhappy, you know. I listened to him a lot, I had compassion for him. We started to go out to talk, at a café, at the sea… We talked a lot.
- I understand, don't worry. I'm very happy for both of you.
- Is that true?
- Yes, of course, believe me. I'm sure you make a very nice couple.

As soon as she left, I threw myself into a chair. It was so strange to think that Greg had found comfort with my sister, almost ridiculous from a first view. It was actually hard for me to imagine them in the arms of one another, but well, if they were happy together...

Around the end of the school year, my parents reminded me they were planning to come to Paris for my graduation. They were very proud because they hadn't even finished high school themselves, and saw that what hadn't been able to do would be good for their children. Not procrastinating, I booked them a room in a good hotel, very close to the school. I wanted to offer them a comfortable stay and allow this occasion to be an unforgettable memory. A little bit embarrassed, they also asked for a second room for Greg and my sister, who had insisted to come along as well and celebrate with me the end of my studies. I would have liked Marc to be there too, as he had been there during my oral exam in first year, but that wasn't possible. He was in Vietnam at the moment and was planning to spend two or three more months there. I really was looking forward to see him again.

The big day had come. We were finally graduating, and it was a friendly and festive evening, during which all my teachers, tutors and fellow students were looking their best. Once the ceremony was over, my family came to hug and congratulate me. It was a moving moment, because it signified the end of a time in my life which would never come again, and also because it meant a new chapter of my life, full of new experiences, was beginning. Greg warmly hugged me. We hadn't talked a lot since our separation and I think we needed to show we still had mutual affection for one another.

- Bravo, Laura.
- Thanks, Greg, and thanks for having come here.

He and my sister looked radiant together. Their bond was clearer to me, and I was invited to their wedding.

- Can I ask you something important for me?
- Of course, little one.
- Do you want to be my bridesmaid?

I was expecting the request, actually, and was ready for it. I accepted, repeating my best wishes for the happiness of the future married couple.

Rodolphe Pardon, without giving me the chance to refuse, had generously invited everybody to have dinner at his place that evening. Jeanne had prepared a big, tasty meal, with which her husband had helped. Sitting at the table between my dad and my landlord, I thought to myself that, two years ago, I definitely wouldn't have imagined spending such a day with my family, my ex-fiancé and my landlord in the centre of the capital city! Only Marc was missing, otherwise it would have been perfect.

- Did you know I have employed your daughter for the summer?
- Really? Aren't you coming back to Biarritz?
- I'll come for a few days, then return here. Mr. Pardon would like me to write his biography! It's actually possible that I'll settle down in Paris.

CHAPTER XVIII

In the end, nobody was surprised that I wanted to stay in Paris. It seemed obvious and logical for someone working in the art field. It was pretty much inevitable.

I only stayed for four days at my parent's place, at the beginning of the summer holidays, before returning to my new employer to do a very different kind of work than over the last several months.

In the apartment, everything had been organised around the writing process. Rodolphe Pardon had prepared, with Jeanne's help, a whole room exclusively for this purpose. There was a large desk, two sofas opposite one other, an armchair facing the window, a big soft rug on the ground, and that was all. We planned to have a two hour session each morning at ten and another one of the same length in the afternoon at half past four. In between, I would have free time. I was definitely looking forward to taking advantage of it, during these summer months, to discover all the museums, to see all the exhibitions and all the movies I could watch. I also now had to think about looking for a job, as once summer was over, it would be time to live entirely independently. Even if I would be living with Marc when he got back, which I very much hoped for though it was still uncertain, life in the capital was so expensive I would absolutely need to be earning my own income to stay there. In the mean time, I had heard Paris was especially pleasant in summer and now was the opportunity to verify it myself.

The first session was a bit chaotic, as we didn't know how to start or how to organise ourselves. After a discussion, we decided to follow our instinct. Rodolphe Pardon would tell me about his life, and I would take notes of all the important elements for the biography. Then, step by step, I would write down a first draft of the story, which could be improved upon later. So finally, after getting ourselves sorted, we could start. My narrator gladly began to recount his life, impatient as he was to share his memories.

- I was born in 1947, just after the war. My parents were educated people, born in Paris, who had become retail traders by looking after my grandfather's – on my mum's side - clothes shop. Since they were both well qualified, they did a good job of running the business, which had been quite poorly managed by my grandparents, and succeeded in earning a tidy profit. So, we all were living well-off, my parents, my sister Jeanne and myself…

My first task was to take notes for all useful pieces of information, and to help me Rodolphe Pardon was speaking very slowly and was stopping after each idea. The two hours planned for this work passed by very quickly, without me noticing it. I still didn't know if I could bring to the table quite what my landlord expected from me, but what I did know was that I was impatiently waiting for the next session, because I was very curious to learn more about the details of his life. In some way, we had inverted our roles, as now he was the one telling me a story and I was the one listening to it like a novel, a saga to discover.

One day I received a call from Marc, who told me he had met a Chinese sculptor during a private viewing in Hong-Kong. As usual, his voice carried me away and I was letting it lead me. I felt as if I had been present with him among the sculptures, in the gallery full of visitors from all over the world. I would have liked to go travelling with him so badly! He asked me what I was doing, and I told him about my landlord's project. He thought it was a very good idea, and that it suited me very well. According to him, I had no reason to doubt my ability to fulfil this mission, and if Mr. Pardon had asked me personally, it meant he thought so too. To finish, he advised me to go and see one of his friends, an essayist, who wrote biographies to earn some extra money and who could give me tips for biography writing. I carefully wrote down the name and contact details, glad to have the chance to get help from an experienced professional writer.

Two weeks had gone by since our first writing session. The pace was a little more intensive, though we were always searching for our bearings during our daily dialogues. Marc's friend, a man of wide knowledge, had given me some precious advice which I now put into practice at each session. I was devouring his essays about human relationships during my free time, as he had insisted on offering me several of his publications, and in exchange asking my opinion about them.

We were beginning to arrive at my narrator's years of puberty, which, after a quiet childhood, was a time of rebellion.

- The family life we had was very structured and organised, but it became restricting to me. I needed to escape from it, to find a little more freedom outside of the home. So I looked for people who had nothing in common with my environment, and I found them.

So I learned Rodolphe had succeeded in opposing the family order like that. He had also been supported by Jeanne who covered him as much as she could, a big sister protectress.

- But my taste of freedom didn't last. My parents were very intelligent people. Instead of punishing me and forbidding me to go out, they considered the situation philosophically. They asked me to express what I was experiencing outside of the house, what it was bringing me, whether I had projects they should take in account. After a few weeks, I didn't feel like escaping from home life anymore. Instead I found the comfort and kindness surrounding me were wisdom's best companions.

We were getting closer to the end of July. Marc confirmed to me he couldn't come back before the end of August. I had to be patient, and it was becoming more and more difficult for me to wait for him without knowing the date of his return. For my taste, as well as just to kill time, I was feeding ravenously on art and culture, and so was filling up my free hours. A few people I had met during my studies invited me out to some receptions and exhibitions, and I went along with pleasure, always careful to maintain this special link with this precious world. A world that could help me to obtain a first contract - at least that's what I was hoping for. A lot of guests knew Marc or knew someone who knew Marc, and everybody seemed to have an idea about our relationship, without really mentioning the subject directly. A memory came to mind during one of these evenings. Marc had talked to me about someone close to him who had had trouble, someone with whom he was very close, because he had even been away for several days to look after that person. Yet I had never met this close friend, nor even heard of them – him or her? Who was it? No one else had ever mentioned this person either. I couldn't imagine asking Marc about this mystery during a simple phone conversation, but I really hoped we could discuss the topic and find out the truth with him at his return.

Time passed by. There were just a few more weeks to go and we were now proceeding much faster in the project. Around mid-August, Rodolphe Pardon announced to me he was going to talk about a very important period in his life, at the time when he and his sister separated to live independently.

-   At first, it was a very strange period for me. I had never lived alone, and I was a little bit confused. I found it hard to get used to it, even if my life was filled with my work…

He told me details about how his daily life had been, and his work, and his more or less involuntarily single situation, because of his shyness among other things. I discovered a little more of him, and came to understand better some aspects of his personality.

We were getting closer to the end of August. Marc would be coming back soon, in one or two weeks at the most. Rodolphe Pardon pressed forward in his life's account. We were now twenty years before I first met him.

\-   I met a young man, through my sister. He was fifteen years old at the time, actually, and was in quite a violent phase of rebellion against his parents, in particular against his father. Jeanne knew his mother, who was a childhood friend she had more or less drifted away from since then. One day, having met again by chance, the young man's mother started to talk to my sister about her son. She said she had had enough - the relationship between her husband and their son was getting worse and becoming unbearable. She explained to my sister, her son was aggressive towards his father and was demean and insult him all the time when she was around. She didn't know what to do. When Jeanne talked to me about it, I felt particularly touched by the story. I don't know why, but I wanted to help him. I think I felt myself capable of bringing the attention and the kindness I had received myself from my own parents to another young man. I had the feeling I could understand him. I was living alone, and even if I didn't have children, it wasn't an obstacle for me to understand their discontent.

The session stopped there. However, I would have gladly kept on going - this young man interested me, and my narrator had emphasised specifically the importance of this period of his life. By helping out to this young man, their relationship might have meant a lot for the young rebel as well as for Rodolphe Pardon. There must have been something in their relationship that had impressed my landlord so much that he wanted to tell me about.

So, it was with impatience that I sat down in the room the next day.

-   I discovered that the young man indeed held a lot of anger for his father. He seemed to have a lot against him, and after several meetings, he confessed to me that his dad never valued him, never complimented him, never congratulated him. In the contrary, he was always making bad comments about his homework and exams at school, about his bad behaviour, about his uninteresting friends…

It was that evening that Marc suddenly announced me that he would be returning in two days. Stirred by the joy of seeing him again soon, I quickly wrote down the arrival time and the flight number. I was very keen on picking him up at the airport, and was already thinking about what I would wear, about the pleasure I would have to be in his arms again.

That same evening, my sister called me too. She wanted to confirm the date of her wedding with Greg, and be sure I could be there that day. So, their story really was serious, and it seemed they were made for one another, according to some family members…

- He was actually very nice young man. Nevertheless, I didn't want him to get too used to talking to me, as it wasn't quite bringing him back to his parents. So I asked my sister what she thought about it. She said, at least when he was able to express himself to me, he came home relaxed and without such aggressiveness towards his mother and father. With that in mind, and with his parents' permission, I was glad to welcome him every evening of the week, after high school - and in fact, he seemed to be regaining interest in school. Slowly, we started trusting each other and I began to better understand his anxiety. He had internalised his father's constant criticisms and put-downs, accepting them as reality, and had entirely lost confidence in himself. He really did have a terrible idea of himself. Imagine, he was unable to accept any compliment anymore, and he almost always expected criticism from me, as if it were inevitable. Given the apparent severity of the problem, I sought advice from a psychologist, who offered to look after the young man. Unfortunately, he never accepted this offer, and we had to put an end to our relationship when he went away for his studies to the other side of Paris.

It now was the day before Marc's return, and I couldn't keep calm, which was annoying Rodolphe Pardon a little bit, as I had trouble staying still. I hadn't spoken to him about my lover, so he didn't know the effort I had been making to keep my tension level, caused by his absence, down and under control. I had an outfit picked out already and I had booked a table in Marc's favourite restaurant as a surprise. I was at once as happy as could be while also very anxious, worrying that he might have changed his mind or that somehow he wouldn't make it back. The sessions went on like a countdown until his return.

- Later I received news about him again, though Jeanne. I learned he was regularly going to dating clubs specialising in sadomasochism. It didn't appear to me he had succeeded in throwing away the bad image he had of himself. Meanwhile, his parents had brutally died in a car crash.

My narrator stopped talking. For a few days now, the personality of this young man Rodolphe Pardon had supported during his puberty had begun to seem more and more familiar to me. For the first time during his account, I dared to interrupt.

- Do you know what he's doing now?
- He's done very well. He's now a furniture trader interior decorator here in Paris. He's very successful and knows a lot of people in the art world.
- Did you ever see him again?
- Yes, actually, for a few years now I have been seeing him regularly, talking with one another again. Jeanne sometimes has him around at her place, too. He also came to see me at the hospital, after my accident. You had just missed him, in fact. He had arrived five minutes or so later, just after you left.

This time I felt no doubt. The young man, it was Marc. I sank into my armchair, suddenly drained of energy, my note book slipping out of my hands. Rodolphe Pardon continued on, still without mentioning his name. Now so curious, I asked a question which had nagged me so long.

- Did this young man finally get to build a family life?
- He got married at twenty-five years old. I was invited at the wedding, Jeanne too. She was a lovely woman, elegant, well mannered, perfect. They seemed very happy together.
- And what happened?
- He simply couldn't rid himself of his demons, despite doing everything he could and even though his wife had shown exemplary patience towards him. She loved him deeply but she couldn't bear his masochist tastes, and all her efforts to steer him away from what she considered a deviant behaviour were in vain. She ended up falling sick. They decided to split up, though she ended up moving into the apartment just below him, which had just become available. He took care of her a lot when she wasn't feeling well. In fact, she had to stay several times at the hospital due to depression.

- And then, he posted an announcement for a room to rent for a student, in exchange for minor services, didn't he?
- That's right, yes.
- And when the student told him she wouldn't return the following year, he asked his friend Rodolphe Pardon to post an announcement too, so that the student would imagine she had found by chance a new room to rent, with similar conditions, is that so?
- Indeed, you're right.
- Why did he do that? Why did he want the student to live at his friend's place?
- To help her to finish her studies without her finding out he was the one helping, because she would have probably not accepted it.
- Why did he want to help her?
- Because he believes in her, But above all, because he's fallen in love with her,
- In that case, why did he never try to see her again when they weren't living together anymore. Why did he always stay away from dinners to which she was invited?
- He didn't want to cut her away from her family, and she had told him she was going to get married. But he always asked his close friends about her, as he knew she was meeting with common friends from time to time.
- And why didn't he tell her this story himself?

- It was my idea actually. I thought it would be easier this way, because the emotion involved can make such a story hard to tell. And in any case, I wanted to write my biography.
- But what about the other woman? And what do you think about the fact that the man and the student are a couple now?
- Well, his ex-wife had divorced him before the student arrived. She met someone else and now lives with her new partner. She thought the student looked like a nice girl, anyway. And as for him, what I can say is that meeting this student made him want to change. He realised he can be loved as he is, which before then he didn't think was possible. He finally went to see a psychiatrist, who he was seeing for about a year, until he left to Asia.
- And now he'll be back tomorrow, and the student is going to see how much he's changed…
- I think she already had the opportunity to see it for herself, during their last day together before he left, just over seven months ago…

Anyway, how about you just call me Rodolphe now?

ISBN for paperback version : 979-10-96121-02-1

Dépôt Légal : juillet 2016